# TALES OF MYSTERY AND SUSPENSE

## KEV CARTER
Copyright

9798642175316
2020

www.fancyacoffee.wix.com/kev-carter-books

# DOG

Panting as it ran, the large Doberman dog moved quickly, its teeth blood stained and blood

splashed on its dark fur around its neck. It ran steady along and then came to a stop by the side of the very busy road. It sat down and waited. The traffic was fierce, fast and roaring past only a few feet away from where it had sat down. Waiting patiently and obediently it sat motionless. Then suddenly it looked up and just ran out onto oncoming traffic. It was hit with such force by the fast travelling car that it was almost cut in half and then spun across into the path of another car. It was killed instantly and obliterated into nothing but bits of flesh and bone, as more cars hit and ran over the carcass. They screeched to a halt as some crashed into others and the chaos began, the road was eventually brought to a standstill. People were getting out of their vehicles and shouting at one another, arguing and throwing their hands in the air as they tried to find out what had happened. Some people got out in a panic and others angry. There was nothing left of the dog, just blood splattered over the cars and ground, bits of its body were scattered and some would never be seen again.

## Eight months earlier.

She always had a smile on her face, a pretty girl and very popular with her friends, long dark hair and a slim figure, she would grow into a fine woman one day. Her father was watching her on the video tape he had put in the recorder. The picture flickered to him of a much happier time when he shot this footage only a year or so before. He had lost his wife and his child on the same night and now he knew why and who was responsible. The law had not helped and seemed to protect the guilty over gaining justice and doing what is right.

She had become more and more distant and more moody. A complete change in character and it worried him and his wife.

When they finally found out about the drugs it was too late, she was hooked and the man who had done it only lived a short distance away. He was a known drug user and got every benefit going. He just played the system and got away with it.

He had broken into an old ladies house and robbed her, but his probation officer had got him off with the "he doesn't know what he is doing, it's not his fault" card. The whole street was livid but he had too many "do well and good" people on his side just letting him get away with things and not seeming to care who he hurt or what crime he committed. He played the innocent victim to them but the whole street knew what he was really like and the evil, nasty bastard he really was.

His wife had her suspicions for a long time as she could see the signs before he could. She confided in him on the night she went out, the night she would not return, the last night he would see her alive. She insisted she go alone because she wanted to make sure she was right, he should've insisted on going with her, he should of made sure she was ok. But she told him she was going on the next

4

night, a Saturday but actually she went on Friday night. He would never understand why she went alone, that answer would never be answered. She left the house to go to her yoga class as normal, or so he thought, she had been going to yoga for over a year, always on a Friday night for an hour, leaving at seven thirty and getting back about nine. They had agreed to go and confront this man about their daughter on Saturday night. But she went alone on Friday.

He would never be sure of what truly happened, but for what he can understand she went round to the house and caught him with their daughter, who was out of her mind on drugs and he was using her like a common prostitute. His wife had an argument and grabbed her daughter, she ran from the house dragging her comatose daughter with her as this man ran after her with a knife, shouting and threatening them both. She managed to get into the car and speed off but lost control and hit an oncoming lorry, they both died in the hospital that night from severe head injuries.

He was told to stay away from this man, The man who had caused the death of his wife and child, then stood there laughing in the street, he was told it would be dealt with, he was told to take counselling, he was told, and told and told. But never helped, not really truly helped. It was never even explained to him what really happened that night. He just had to piece it all together himself. He talked to neighbours and other people who knew this man. Some were helpful, some were afraid and many were very aggressive and rude. No charges seem to be coming and yet again this drug addict was protected by a society that seems to victimise the innocent and protect the guilty.

He grieved and he hurt and he wept, he suffered and he sobbed, he lost sleep and he lost weight. Then one day he awoke and had the plan he was going to put into practice, a plan that if worked would rid this planet of a despicable and evil drug taking human being. A plan that would not implicate him in the least and a plan that he knew he could do. He had read up on it and researched it meticulously. He was sure he could do it and was sure it would

6

work if he could get the right one. He searched and h̶ ... y

careful to hide his identity when he finally got the ɑ

powerful animal and he now had to train it right. A w

what he was using, a whistle the dog could hear but not hɩ

no one would know of the commands he was giving this ɑ

trained it every day, not letting anyone see the dog at any tim

trained it in the house, he took it out in the back of his van to a

away field with no around as he commanded and trained it what tʊ

do, the commands he gave it with his whistle, one blow to stop, two

to run, three to attack and so forth. He put into practice what he had

read and worked hard and determinedly at his task. It took some

months but he was now seeing progress. No one even knew he had

this dog, no one ever knew it existed. Early hours of the morning

he walked the dog to where it was to do its job, to execute its task.

He got it familiar with the surroundings when there was no one else

about, it got the area covered it was working and thinking just as he

wanted it to, just as he was commanding and training it to. Walking

it down the street and walking it where he wanted it to run. He sat it at the top of the street and walked away then blew his whistle, the dog came as commanded. It sat as commanded, and then he blew his whistle again and it ran as commanded. He was making good progress and he was getting nearer the time to execute his plan.

He doubled checked on how to do this and began to starve the dog, to get it more aggressive and to attack on command. He put a lot of effort in training it to go for the throat. To rip and tear and pull and rip, it learnt well and he was doing a good job.

The night was clear and it was time for a dry run, he took the dog to the street and left it to sit motionless, there was no one around and he was very careful not to be seen. He walked away and placed himself up on the hill side only a few minutes' walk from where he left the animal. He took out his binoculars and peered through them, he could just make out the dog by the street lights but it was not very good, he should've got some night vision goggles for the job. But for now this would do. He took out the dog whistle and blew it, the distance was great but the dog heard it and moved off, he whistled again and smiled as all his hard work

8

seemed to be working. He watched as the dog ran exactly where he wanted it to through the commands of the whistle, he again blew and made it sit. He looked around and one last blow ran the dog across the road. He was pleased and ran down to meet the dog and take it secretly home. The exercise had been a success.

He still worked on the attack and still made sure he would get it right, he only had one chance of this working and didn't want to mess it up. He knew it would not bring his wife or child back, but at least it would rid the world of a piece of scum, a degenerate reprobate of a human being. He had more remorse over the dog then he did over this man.

He now had to solve one more problem and he was ready, ready to avenge his wife and child and rid the world of an evil. This is how he saw it and this is what kept him sane about what he was going to do. The problem he had was getting the man alone and giving his dog time to do the job it had been trained for. He needed it to be a busy time, he had considered doing it quietly and then disposing of the dog himself but that would've sparked an investigation. This way he thought it would be better for people to see what happened and the demise of the animal with no trace.

It was Friday and a busy time, he had spent weeks watching the house and it was difficult to get any routine on this man as he was very random and irregular, people came to his house and seemed to stay for days and then leave, and he sometimes didn't come out at all. But he had noticed on Fridays he seemed to leave the house and come back around mid evening. This was then going to be the time. He went to the hillside and sat looking down with his binoculars, he saw the door open and the man leave, he had no emotion and just breathed in and then out slowly. If he was right in about an hour the man would return and not be seen all weekend, he thought he must be going to his supplier on Fridays. He waited forty-five minutes then looked down at the fierce doberman dog sat like a sentry next to him. He felt sorry for the dog, touched its head then sent him off down to do its job.

The dog trotted down and followed the instruction from the whistle only it could hear, giving it directions all the time.

Eventually it reached the street and walked up across the road from this man's house. It stopped and sat patiently waiting for its next command. It did not look at anyone and no one really paid it much attention. Or if they did they were weary of it and gave it a wide berth.

Watching through the binoculars he waited and waited, eventually he bolted into action, here he was, the man walking down the street, the man who was responsible for his wife and child being dead, responsible for causing hurt and distress to the decent people in the street, the man who did not care who he hurt or what lives he ruined. The man who groomed young girls and got them hooked on drugs then used them like common prostitutes. This was his last day on the planet but he just didn't know it yet.

He walked up the street and looked half asleep, he was obviously under some influence of the drugs he took; the dog watched him and waited. It watched and listened. Watching through his binoculars he took the whistle and put it in his mouth, licking his lips before he did, they were dry and he could feel his

11

breath getting heavier, his heart began to beat faster. The man was at his door, he struggled to get the key in the latch, but did it and as soon as the door was opened the whistle was blown to attack, attack, and attack.

The dog with lightening speed ran across the road and pounced through the air, knocking the man down and into his house, he turned and looked into the fierce eyes of this powerful dog that had been conditioned into a killing machine, as trained and as commanded it went for his throat and ripped it out with ease and speed. Then again it tore and ripped at his neck. The blood pumped out like a fountain as the jugular was severed and torn from its bedding. He was dead in a matter of minutes. There was nothing anyone could do, people screamed and ran away, some looked out of their windows and watched the dog finish its job. Then without warning it backed out of the house, and fled off down the street. The few people that were about were in a panic and didn't know what to do. From the hillside the dog was being commanded to go to the busy road side. It panted as it ran and then stopped and sat next to the road, waiting its next command.

"Thank you" he said as he blew the last command and the dog ran out into the oncoming traffic getting annihilated as it did.

He slowly stood and went back home. He disposed of all the evidence he had of even owning a dog, he sat in his chair looking at the picture of his wife and his daughter. And then burst into tears, the time for healing had begun....


The End

# CHARLIE WALL

"I do not want to go, it is just not my scene Jessica" Trevor told her as he sat on the bed looking at the carpet and waiting for the answer he knew would come from his girlfriend who was in the bathroom getting ready.

"You are so bloody boring, we are going and you are not going to show me up" she came striding back into the room. Walked past him and went to the fitted white wardrobe next to the bed. She was dressed just in her underwear which at one time he would have found attractive and sexy but now it just didn't bother him at all.

"It is at a bloody air field" he stated not looking up from the carpet.

"It was an air field, it is now being renovated into a function complex and we are going to support the project, it is a social gathering" so just stop moaning and get ready.

She pulled out a small dress and held it up to inspect it, then started to put it on. He sighed out and fell back onto the bed laying flat looking up at the ceiling. They had been together for over a year but the last few months it had all changed. Ever since she got the job, made her new friends, started to go out with colleagues from work at the weekend.

"You mean you just want to show off in front of people" he said.

"Oh shut up, you are not going to humiliate me again; you just do not fit in anywhere do you. Everyone is taking their partner, which is the only reason you are coming, so try and blend in. Talk to people, not like last time it was so bloody embarrassing" she looked at herself in the full length mirror and turned to inspect her dress and how it looked.

"I have nothing in common with your new friends; they all talk bollocks and are extroverts"

"They have fun, they are interesting and they make the effort, I work with these people I have to make the effort, and not only that I have some fun as well"

"They are false and do not give a shit about you, they are self absorbed wankers"

"I do not know how the fuck we ever got together do you know that, what the hell do we have in common?" she stated and strode back into the bathroom.

"We did, and we were happy, until you met your new friends now it is all them and not us"

"They have fun, they want to do things what the hell do you want to do, you are just a boring sad idiot and I have no idea what the hell I saw in you to be honest"

"Thank you very much" he said getting up off the bed and didn't hear what she said after that. He went down stairs and started to put his shoes on.

She came down the stairs about ten minutes later, and then looking at herself again in the hall mirror she checked her little bag to make sure she had her makeup and essentials. She walked past Trevor as if he was not here and headed for the car. Trevor locked the door and followed.

They didn't speak for a time then he asked a question he knew the answer too already.

"So how long does this go on for?

"Until it does, until it finishes so just try and not show me up and be a boring bastard, I work with these people and we all get along great so I will not let you spoil it for me" she pulled down the visor and looked at herself in the mirror checking her lipstick was straight and she looked her best. He shook his head and thought of how much she had changed. She was all over him when she was unemployed and he was taking her out and paying for her, he even moved her in to his rented house. Then she got this job and her own money and she changed. Now she spent her money on herself, he knew it was only a matter of time before she left him. He was not stupid and could see it there just waiting to happen. He drove along and thought about it, thought about what to do. He was not heartless and remembered when they first met how happy they seemed. But how times change he sighed to himself and gritted his teeth, he knew he was going to hate every minute of this and feel out of place. They didn't speak again until they got there; he drove up the road and through two large iron gates. Then down the road to where they could see the tables set out and people stood chatting, holding drinks, being sociable. He looked out across the field and the runway. He looked across to see the old control tower. He knew this place has been active in the war, he imagined for a moment the planes taking off and heading over to defend the country against enemy planes. It made him feel better somehow, made him feel proud. They parked up where the other cars were outside a hanger type building. Jessica is looking out of the window, a big smile on her face and excitement in her actions as she waves to someone. She cannot wait to get out of the car and dash over to three men and two women who are stood together.

She blended in immediately and he was left to go get some drinks. He looked round and could see what looked an old mess hall, he walked over to the make shift bar. Three tables put together with overpriced drinks on them where he got Jessica her favourite and he just asked for some water. On his way back out he saw an old man holding a sweeping brush. He nodded to him and Trevor smiled and nodded back saying.

"Lovely place, lot of character and important history, it should be preserved"

"It will be" the old man smiled at him and slowly walked away.

Trevor went out and handed Jessica her drink, she took it without even looking at him. She laughed at something one of her new friends said and the others all laughed in the same way. Extroverts and false empty people did not interest him at all. He was saddened to think she had become one of them people.

It went on and he was left out, being made to feel, and looking an unimportant outsider. She eventually turned to him and under her breath told him to cheer up, then smiled across at another man and waved. A couple came along and she fell over herself laughing and greeting them, they were just so false it was embarrassing to him. The two women chatted and the man who she had greeted as Gavin turned to him.

"You not drinking?" he asked looking down at Trevor's glass of water.

"No, I am driving" he said politely.

"Aw, I see, well one won't hurt will it.

"I would rather not" They didn't like each other that was obvious already, but this arrogant man in front of him was going to still talk and try and make him feel uncomfortable.

"You won't get anywhere if you don't take chances, live a bit; we are on this planet for a good time not a long time. What is it you do, what is your line of work?"

Before Trevor could answer there was a burst of laughter from Jessica and this woman. Another man then joined in cutting Trevor dead as if he wasn't even there and turned his back on him.

Turning away he looked out across the airfield and again imagined the fighter planes that must have taken off from her during the war. The brave men who fought and defended the country, he was rocked out of his daydream by a rough nudge to his shoulder.

20

"Hay you with us, you look miles away" this ignorant and annoying man had come back to try and humiliate him again.

"I am here yes; I am just imagining what it must have been like in the war here, what we owe the men and woman who use to operate from here"

"Oh fuck not another one, how many times do your sort need to be told, move on, the bloody war is over and always will be, there is potential here for development, we have invested a lot of money and time into it, it cannot fail, and will not fail. Who gives a fuck about the war, no one fought a war for me" the man took a drink from his glass and looked at Trevor with distaste and dislike.

"They fought a war for everyone, you would not be here if it was not for them" Trevor defended and could see Jessica glaring at him from the corner of his eye.

"Bollocks, you have no imagination and no idea what you are talking about" he turned away and Jessica came over to Trevor saying under her breath but still outward looking calm.

"What the fuck are you doing, just fucking stop being a twat, he is my boss and you are showing me up, for fuck sake" she stared at him then turned and started to talk to this man who had turned away. He put his arm round her and whispered something into her ear. Glancing over at Trevor as he did, Jessica burst out laughing and Trevor had, had enough of the false humiliating situation. He looked away and across the air strip. Then down towards the old hanger on the other side. He saw a man sat by himself on a chair. He was a young looking man in his early twenties. He was wearing a brown leather sheepskin jacket with fur edges. Just sat there looking out across the field that use to be the runway, Trevor looked round and could see people had moved away from him, he was isolated as usual. Jessica was chatting and flirting and showing off with everyone she could.

Trevor slowly walked out and towards the young man. On approaching him, the young man turned and stared at him for a moment then smiled and nodded in a friendly fashion.

Trevor got closer and smiled back; he could see the man was dressed in World War II fighting clothes. The jacket he was wearing was worn and hung off him like it was too large. Trevor got close and noticed another wooden chair next to the man and gestured to it to ask if he could sit.

"Yes of course old man, sit yourself down" the voice was young but spoke like it was old. He smiled a friendly smile at Trevor who felt at ease and sat down next to him. He glanced over to the party going on less than a hundred yards away. He didn't like those people and was happy he was out of the extrovert area.

"Thank you just need to get away you know" Trevor said nodding over to the others.

"I understand that, not one for big crowds myself"

"Love your outfit, very authentic, must've cost a lot" Trevor said looking at the man's dress.

"Thank you, it does the trick when needed"

"I was wondering earlier on, just how many planes have taken off from here to defend our country, the Hurricanes, the Spitfires.

23

Must have been amazing but totally frightening, we owe just a huge debt to the men and women who gave their all and more defending our country" Trevor said it with genuine heartfelt honesty, he was real and what he said was real.

"I take it not many people think like you these days" he said looking over to the party area.

"No and it is so wrong, greed has taken over everything, money is all people are bothered about and image, false image, makes me sad to be honest"

"Well the world will become what it will become, but it is nice to hear such words from you I must say" he turned and smiled at Trevor.

"So you here for a reconstruction or Remembrance Day thing something like that?" Trevor asked admiring his outfit once again and smiling in admiration of it.

"No, not really I often sit here and chat with whoever wants to and whoever can chat" he smiled and then turned to Trevor, his eyes were the well lived eyes but his age didn't compliment them.

24

Trevor looked over at the other people and saw a few looking at him and giggling he ignored them and turned back.

"My name is Trevor by the way" he said.

"Wall, Charlie Wall, pleased to meet you and greet you"

"Likewise Charlie"

"So you like the old airfield then, you have not been here before?" Charlie asked.

"No, I have not to be honest I didn't really know it was still active, apparently they are going to do some development here, but I think it should be preserved and restored to remind people of the sacrifices made for them, this is where they should be bringing kids from school. Showing them our history, how the men in them planes held off the Lufwaffe, how we won the battle of Britain, how we stood alone against the might of the German Air Force, how if those brave pilots had not done what they did the war would've been over." Trevor said what he said with passion and genuine admiration.

"That is a wonderful thing to hear, not very often do you hear such words these days, but be assured this is always going to be an airfield" Charlie smiled at him.

"I hope so, it would be tragic if a bunch of pricks like that tore it down and made money out of it just to satisfy their bloody greed and egos, they have no bloody respect"

"Like I said it will always be an airfield. Have you ever flown Trevor?"

"No I cannot say I have, just think how it would be up in a Spitfire or Hurricane, the Merlin engine roaring and pulling you along through the sky. I did go to Duxford once with the school when I was a kid and saw a few Spitfires fly along with the Lancaster Bomber, what a great day out that was, that distinctive sound a Merlin makes, bloody amazing"

"Yes it is a great aircraft, the Hurricane is stronger more robust but not as fast in the air. The Spit was a dream to fly and was a good match for the Messerschmitt 109's"

"You know it is a pleasure to talk to someone who understands and has the same admiration for a change Charlie" Trevor looked over again to the party, he saw Jessica staring at him with a fuming look on her face, but at this moment he didn't care.

They chatted for a good while longer and Trevor was immersed in conversation like he had not been for a long time, to finally find someone who understood and had the same opinion as himself. He eventually could hear the chatter and some laughter coming his way from the party area. He sighed and knew he would have to be heading back over soon.

"Don't worry Trevor you can come visit here anytime, we can have long chats about the war and anything else really, like I said this will always be an airfield so don't worry about that" Charlie said and then glanced over Trevor's shoulder.

Trevor turned round and saw Jessica marching towards him with a scowl on her face. Standing he looked at her and she started to shout at him instantly.

"What the fuck is wrong with you, have you gone out of your tiny mind, you have made me look like a right fucking idiot"

"What are you on about, I am here just chatting with Charlie" he turned and saw the chair was empty and no one around. He felt strange and looked up as he heard the distinctive noise of a roaring Merlin engine fly past him but he could see no plane.

"You have been sat here talking to yourself for an hour, everyone laughing at you; you are a fucking idiot and an embarrassment. Just go home and stay there, you have tried to deliberately ruin this for me. I told you how important this was, if this development doesn't go through they will be getting shut of some of their work force" she shook her head and looked at him with hate in her eyes, she prodded him and he looked down at her and he knew at that moment it was all over.

"I was chatting with Charlie, he was sat just here didn't you see him?"

"There was no one and everyone saw you talking to yourself you fucking freak, just fuck off and I am getting a lift back, so
28

don't expect me home, it's over goodbye" she stormed off and he saw her walk straight up to Gavin, he gave him a little sarcastic wave and smile.

Trevor took a deep breath he had seen this coming and should not have been surprised. It still hurt and he looked away. He searched again for Charlie but could not see him anywhere. He walked away and out through the large building where he saw the old man sweeping up again, as he walked past, the man said, without looking up from his broom.

"You saw Charlie then?"

"What, yes where is he?" Trevor turned and asked. The old man just smiled and nodded over to an old framed picture on the far wall then he carried on sweeping.

Trevor went over to it and saw it was the old photo of the squadron who used to fly from here, it was dated 1940 and he looked at the faces of the young men there in their brown sheepskin jackets. He then noticed a face he recognised, his heart missed a beat. He looked round but the old man had finished sweeping and was gone. Looking back he looked down to the names printed below and one name glared out at him. "Charlie Wall" He went home with a strange calm; he was initially upset about what had happened but now he seemed alright, glad even. He smiled it had turned out to be a good party after all. The next few days were silent and he heard nothing, she had come when he was out and got her things, not even leaving him a note. The following week he heard the deal had fallen through, it was in the local paper about a development in the local air field that had collapsed and the company behind it had to lay off people because of it. He ignored her calls and blocked her number. He knew she wanted to come back, he knew she would be all over him again and he knew it would all change as soon as she got another job. No, he was better off alone, he had plans today to go down to the airfield. He was hoping to have another chat with his new friend Charlie Wall......

The End

Kev Carter

# VENTRILOQUIST

The office was not clean but it was well worked, the place had been decorated a long time ago and from that day on, just touched up occasionally.

The walls had posters and framed programs decorating them from performers and acts from the stage and screen, most gone and long forgotten.

He sat there, calm and expressionless, a large suitcase by his side, he was dressed sensibly and tidy, there didn't seem like anything special about him and no one would pay him a second look in the street.

That was just how he liked it, he sat on a wooden chair and waited patiently, his right hand resting on the suitcase and looking forward.

He had been there almost an hour now and had no response from the office in front of him. His appointment was for 2.00pm, he had arrived at 1.45pm. The young annoying girl the agent called a secretary had told him to wait and then gone into the office. She was still in there, he had heard giggling and the odd moan. He paid it no attention at this time but it had been locked away in his memory. He looked down at the suitcase and then back at the door.

Another twenty minutes passed before the door opened and a bitchy looking young girl came out adjusting her hair as she did, this was the secretary of sorts who ignored him and walked out the other door. He looked at the agent's door which had been left open, he could see inside an empty desk, a moment later a large overweight man came from the side and sat at this desk, he looked up and caught sight of him, he gestured him to come in as he looked at his watch.

Calmly he stood and took the suitcase in with him, he closed the door behind him and stood in front of this obnoxious man, who looked up and then looked him up and down.

"Ok let me see what you have got, I am a busy man so don't be offended if I send you on your way, what you have to understand is I have seen it all and heard it all, if you have nothing special then you might as well leave now, I have managed the best and know what works and what doesn't." His voice was unfriendly and his body language matched it perfectly. He leaned back in his chair and took a deep breath clasped his hands behind his head and waited, the sweat stains were under his arms and the odor followed.

"Thank you for seeing me, I think I will show you something that you will be very interested in and maybe not seen before"

"What is your name by the way?" The agent snapped.

"Geoff"

"Do you not have a stage name; bloody Geoff is not going to get you anywhere is it?"

Smiling, Geoff placed the suitcase on the floor and carefully opened it, he pulled out the perfect looking dummy and held it in his right hand as he stood up straight again. He placed his foot on the small wooden chair in front of him and sat the dummy on his knee; he put his hand in the hole in the back and got his hand on the controls ready.

It was a pristine condition ventriloquist dummy, wide eye's, just oversize head but not too much to stand out, dressed in a suit and bright polished shoes, the overall effect looked proficient and professional.

"Let me stop you there before you begin, I have seen these acts before and to be honest they are dead as a dodo, drinking water as you say the alphabet, trying to get the audience to concentrate on the doll instead of your mouth movement, it is all old stuff and has been seen before, you have to be very skilled and have something new for it to work so you better be good and I mean fucking good"

Smiling Geoff took a deep breath and looked the agent straight in the eye, the doll seemed to click into life and the eyes moved round the head turned to inspect the room then it fixed its gaze on the agent, for a moment it just stared at him then the expression changed and the eye brows lifted and the mouth opened.

"Let me introduce myself because it is me you will want not him" the dummy spoke in a very audible voice and there was no muffle or distortion whatsoever, just a very sensible but little menacing tone. Geoff's mouth never moved a fraction and he was

34

still and silent as the dummy spoke.

The dummy smiled at the agent, then the head turned to Geoff who looked back at it and smiled, the dummy smiled back and then looked at the agent once more.

"Get on with the act, I am a busy man" He said pulling his hands back onto the desk as he leaned forward.

"Ok, ok let's get on with it, can you please give this man a deck of cards Geoff" the dummy instructed and from nowhere Geoff produced a deck of cards in his left hand and threw then on the table in front of the agent.

"Open the pack, see it is a new pack and then shuffle them," the dummy insisted, this was done without any enthusiasm, "Ok now you pick a card, and place it on the table in front of you," this was done as instructed.

"I know you are not yet impressed but just wait and see" the dummy did all the talking and Geoff said nothing. His mouth never twitched, and there was not even movement in his throat, the agent watched and noticed this and knew this man was very good.

"Ok your card was what?" the dummy asked baring its teeth in a macabre smile.

"Three of diamonds" The agent said looking at Geoff and trying to see any movement whatsoever in his throat or lips.

"Turn the card over then" The dummy insisted.

This was done and it was blank, the agent looked up quickly, he knew it was a trick but had not seen it done at this distance before, he looked at Geoff.

"Magic with a dummy?" the agent said.

"Look at the cards please" the dummies voice had become stern and serious.

Flicking through the rest of the deck he was amazed they were all the three of diamonds, he picked at them and rubbed them to see if they were trick cards in anyway, he had just shuffled them and he had just looked at them seeing they were a normal deck.

"Cute trick, is that your best one?"

"Oh no sir we do a song and dance act too, but let me ask you to take something from your pocket and I will show you some magic"

"You need some rapport between you and the dummy, some interaction, banter, you need to speak to each other" the Agent insisted.

"We will come to that later" Geoff said.

"Yes we will. I do not like him speaking when I do" the dummy came back with perfectly.

"I will let him impress you, then we will go into a comedy act as well" Geoff began.

"I am the one who impresses you see and then he comes back with some jokes" the dummy carried on to perfection.

"We have many routines, some funny, some amazing, and some that will just leave you for dead" Geoff smiled.

"Right, but before that, take something from your pocket and let me show you some bloody magic" the dummy insisted looking at the Agent intensely.

"What do you want from my pocket?"

"Any fucking thing, just take something out?" it snapped.

"Calm down and watch your language" Geoff said looking at his dummy.

Reaching into his pocket the agent took out his wallet and placed it on the desk in front of him. He looked up at Geoff and waited.

"Hey, it's me who is doing the fucking trick" the dummy spat.

Turning his attention to the dummy the agent stared into its eyes.

"Ok that's good, look at me and I will show you some real magic"

They stared at each other for a moment then the dummy let out a hideous laugh and rocked back and forth on Geoff's knee.

"What, what is so fucking funny?" the agent snapped at Geoff.

"Ok first let me open your wallet, looking down he saw the wallet was opened and spread out on the desk, he looked up at Geoff aghast, sticking out of the inside pocket was a playing card, he took this out and turned it over. It was the three of diamonds.

"Let me close the wallet for you" The dummy laughed and the

wallet snapped shut by itself, the agent threw himself back in the chair and the startled look on his face caused the dummy to mockingly laugh at him.

"What the fuck is going on" the agent demanded.

"Well this is just the start, it gets really good in a bit" the dummy said turning its head to Geoff who turned his head and they looked at each other. Then they both looked at the wide eyed and slightly nervous agent who was backing into his chair as far as he could.

"Are you OK? This is just the start, or is it too much for you?" The dummy asked calmly

"You are not moving your lips, there is nothing there whatsoever, that is not a fucking dummy is it" the agent came forward in his chair looking at the dummy in front of him, looking back into his eyes.

"Boo" the dummy shouted and the eyes opened wide and the teeth were bared into a snarl as the face became evil looking for a moment, the agent jumped back in fear but the dummy stayed motionless.

Geoff took the dummy off his knee and placed it on the table laid flat on its back, he undid some velcro fastening round the arms and pulled these off and he did the same with the legs. Then the head was pulled out from the neck to revel a wooden ventriloquist dummy, lifeless and in pieces.

He sat down on the chair in front of him and watched the agent carefully prod the wooden dummy on his desk. He picked up a leg and tapped it, seeing it was made of wood, he prodded the chest and felt it was also solid wood.

He was amazed at the skill of this man's Ventriloquist skill, he had no idea how he had done the trick with the wallet but he saw the wallet move by itself he was sure of that.

"You are good, son, I will give you that, very good, but it takes a lot more than just being clever to make it big, you need help and I can give you that help, you were right to come to me" The agent smiled for the first time, but it did not change Geoff's still expression.

"What about me?" the voice came from the dummy on his desk.

"You throw your voice very well I must say you are good at this" The agent said looking at Geoff then the dummy and back to Geoff.

"Well it took a lot of understanding to be able to do it, it took me a long time to be able to express it and tame it, and understand it" Geoff said.

"What do you mean tame it? I need you in control you have to be in control"

"I am in control, perfect control at all times, you are in for a treat and a real show of magic soon. Believe me, something that has never been done before."

"You make me nervous I don't know why, but you do" The agent suddenly put up his guard and looked deep into Geoff's eyes but saw nothing, nothing like emotion at all.

"Well I know you are a busy man and must see a lot of people, I know you have a casting couch and I know you abuse young girls,

41

I know you use people and mercilessly ruin lives, I know much more about you then you can imagine with your narrow, bigoted, selfish, pathetic and filthy mind."

Geoff had become frightening to him, he could not look him in the eye anymore and turned away, he tried to stand but could not he fought to get out of his chair but could not move.

"Get out; get the fuck out of my office"

"As you can see, like I said, I am in control and you will now see some real magic."

The agent's heart raced, he was petrified, he could not move and he could do nothing about it. Looking at the dummy on his desk he thought he saw movement. He looked again and his eyes widened, the left arm moved, it moved by its self, the fingers stretched out and the whole arm flinched. He stared at Geoff who was looking intensely back at him with a slight, evil smile on his face.

The arm twitched and the hand stretched out and pulled itself across the desk to the second arm, he watched as the arm moved and took hold of the other arm locking it back into place in the torso of the dummy, the second arm reached out and the dummy sat up, pulling the legs back into the joints and locking them into place. The legs and arms were now both locked in and the hands reached down for the head, lifting it up and slotting it back into the neck. The head quickly spun round and stared with wide eyes and mouth open in a snarl at the agent, who was paralyzed with fear as he witnessed the unbelievable spectacle in front of him. He gulped and swallowed looking back at Geoff.

"My young sister came to you some time ago, she was very talented, a superb singer, nice polite and very naïve, do you remember what you said to her?" Geoff asked him.

"Do you remember her?" The dummy shouted as its head shook in anger as it did so.

"No, no I don't know," The agent could not move he was riveted to his chair with fear and felt the wetness trickle down his leg as he wet himself.

"You said you would do your best for her, you said she would go far, you would take her under your wing, look after her" Geoff continued in a quiet composed voice.

"Please, what do you want?" shaking he could do nothing as he had never felt such fear or terror running through his bones. The dummy was staring at him and tilting its head to one side as it did, the menacing look it gave him sent him cold.

"She trusted you", Geoff continued, "and you abused her, Cynthia Bothemly is her name, you said you would get her a much better stage name, all she had to do was trust you, she was sixteen, just sixteen"

The face of the agent turned to confusion then his eyes widened as he remembered the girl and how he took advantage of her, he thought she was a run away and took full advantage of the situation as he always does.

The dummy turned its head and looked at Geoff for a moment, and then it spun back with a snapping sound to stare at the agent once again before saying.

"You took advantage, you abused and did so much damage

you will never know you filthy bastard, I will be watching you and I will be coming for you." The laugh that followed was something that instantly imprinted itself on his mind and brain.

Geoff stood up, picked up the dummy and placed it back into the suitcase. He took the deck of cards from the desk and put these in his pocket as he looked down at the petrified man looking up at him from the chair.

"Don't call us, we will be calling on you" he said and with that he turned and left the office.

Silence followed and the shaking was uncontrollable. For a long minute he sat there looking at the door that was closed behind the man who had just left his office. Eventually he shouted out to his secretary.

"Emma, Emma in here now"

Moments later the young girl came in and walked to the desk looking very confused at her boss shaking in the chair with a wet stain on his pants.

"Yes sir?" she asked.

"The man who has just left with a dummy, suitcase whatever it was, did you see him, did you get his address and name, who was he?" he spluttered out the questions and waited impatiently for the answers.

"You have had no visitors all afternoon sir" she said confused somewhat.

"You showed the man in girl, what are you talking about, you took his details and made the appointment" he shouted.

"Please sir I am confused, there has been no one here all afternoon as I have not taken any bookings sir" the girl was genuinely upset and confused and he realized she must have been brain washed or something.

"Oh get out you silly little bitch, get out and stay out"

She rushed from the room crying and bewildered, upset and confused. He looked round and didn't know what to do, he remembered the girl Cynthia Bothemly. He remembered taking her to a hotel room with promises of stardom and important meetings with record producers. He remembered getting her drunk and raping her, he remembered her tears and how it turned him on even more when she fought him off, or at least tried to fight him off. This happened a long time ago and she just disappeared. He put it down to one more notch to his collection and paid it no more notice, he had sick friends who always would give him perfect alibis and had the security of some powerful people who scratched his back, in return for a supply of young hopefuls who would do anything for the chance of stardom.

He stood up and looked out of the window, searching the street outside; he turned and rubbed his mouth with the back of his hand. Breathing heavy he looked round then left the office, he stormed past the desk where the young girl was still sobbing, and he paid her no notice and dashed out of the door. He rushed to his car and got in. He checked the back seat and looked around like some crazed lunatic, checking every corner, every person he saw. The fear within him rose and he started the car. He pulled away and headed off down the street, looking in his mirror as he did.

He drove quickly his eyes searching everywhere as he did; he drove home and dashed into his modest house. Locking the door behind him he went into the living room going to the window and looked out of it, up and down the street, across his drive and everywhere he could see. He ran up stairs and got changed out of his clothes. He dashed about, packing a suitcase, just throwing things in. He came down stairs and into the living room, taking a bottle of whiskey from the side board he poured himself a glass, gulping it down straight away, he poured another one.

He went and sat down to try and steady himself a little. Had he just witnessed what he saw? Did he imagine it? Was he dreaming? The questions flooded into his head as he sat back into his chair and took a deep breath.

He tried to steady himself and then sighed out, he must be safe here, and no one could know where he lived. He had friends to stay with until it was over, he knew some people who could sort problems out and they always delivered. Nasty people who asked no questions and break limbs for a living, he would hire a few of these and would not be bothered again, yeah that is it, he would get this sorted out.

The thoughts made him feel better and he relaxed back blowing air out of his lungs and sighing. He sat up and rubbed his face then he saw it, a single card on his coffee table, the three of diamonds.

He froze and started to whimper uncontrollably not taking his eyes off the card on the table. He shook and felt the emptiness in his stomach.

"You see, what you do not realize is, we have been watching you for a long time, we know where you live, where you go, your habits your hideouts" it was the voice of the dummy and it was coming from the arm chair behind him.

He dare not look and could not muster the courage to stand.

"Please leave me alone" was all he could say in a weak scared voice.

"I bet those were her words exactly weren't they, please leave me alone, please stop, please it hurts, please do not hit me, please stop touching, please, please, please"

Geoff walked into the room, from where, he didn't see, he looked over to him but didn't move his head only his eyes.

Geoff looked at him with hate in his eyes, standing in front of him he just looked down and stayed motionless.

"What do you want? What can I do to make you go away?" the agent pleaded. Geoff didn't speak it was the dummy that answered from the chair.

"What you did was disgusting, what you do is vile and degrading, you ruin people's lives and get away with it because you have powerful friends. Well every dummy has its day and today its mine" the laugh that followed chilled his blood and he shook even more.

Geoff went to the side and took the three quarter full bottle of whiskey, he came and put it in front of the agent, he signaled for him to take a drink of it. Nervously he did as he was instructed.

"Drink it all, the whole fucking bottle" Geoff demanded.

"All of it, you drink all of it" the voice from the chair added.

"I take it you got Cynthia drunk, I take it you slapped her
50

about a bit too" Geoff said with anger in his voice. Without warning he slapped the agent across the face reeling him back in pain and surprise.

"Hurts, doesn't it?" The voice from the chair shouted out.

"Drink that fucking bottle now, you piece of shit" Geoff said loudly.

The bottle was drunk quickly and he almost made himself sick as he drank it, he gulped and retched a bit, but fear made him do it.

"All of it, you drink all of it" the voice screeched from the chair.

He coughed and spluttered but managed it eventually; Geoff took the bottle from him and placed it on the coffee table saying.

"You feel better now do you, more relaxed, a bit more helpless, more vulnerable, less able to resist?"

"More of the drunken, dirty, filthy pig you are" the voice shouted from the chair.

"Have you noticed the rapport we have now, more interaction wouldn't you say" Geoff added. He walked over to the side and took another bottle of whiskey and threw it at his helpless scared victim in front of him.

"Now you get to drink that one as well" the dummy laughed.

Shaking his head the agent tried to plead with Geoff but it was no good the bottle was thrust in front of him and he was made to drink it.

"I want that bottle drank as well, because I want you to feel as helpless and as scared as Cynthia did, do you remember what you did to her?"

"Drink, and don't spill a drop" the voice bellowed out from the arm chair in a mockingly way with a giggle and evil snarl.

"I will give you anything you want, money I can get you money" the agent pleaded once more, but nothing he could say would change anything that was obvious to him now.

"Promises, you are so good at making promises, but you don't deliver do you? You just manipulate and take advantage, you bully and hurt."

"You need to be taught a lesson you see" the voice from the

chair rang in his ears.

"Drink the fucking whisky" Geoff shouted and stared with angry eyes at him.

The agent began to take drinks from the bottle, he was feeling sick, ill and he was petrified. The alcohol was taking effect and he could feel his ability to perform being taken from him, his body was not responding to what he wanted it to do. He took another mouthful and dribbled it down his front.

"Time to get the rope I think" the dummy said loudly.

"Rope?" the agent said slurring his speech as he did.

"Yes you must have some in fact I know you do, because you sometimes tie young girls up don't you, go and get the rope from your kitchen cupboard I will wait here, but don't be long.

"Don't keep us waiting now will you" the dummy added.

Without knowing why, the agent staggered to his feet, Geoff staring at him the entire time. Wobbling to the kitchen, he went to the cupboard and pulled out a rope, he felt sick and dizzy but by some strange force he did as he was commanded.

When he came back into the room, Geoff had the dummy on his knee again and they both looked at him, it was the same pose he had taken in the office earlier.

"Tie a loop in the end of the rope and feed the other end through it, throw that over the wooden beam above you" the dummy commanded.

It was done, swaying on the spot the agent waited.

"Take another drink" Geoff insisted.

As he did he watched the dummy staring at him with wide eyes and a grin on its face.

"Take a chair and place it under the rope, then stand on it, wrap the rope round your neck tight, then tie it round the rest of the rope so you are secure" the dummy's voice was mesmerizing and had to be obeyed.

This was done, and the agent was drunk helpless and very unsteady on the chair. The rope was tight round his neck and secured well.

"What you have to realise is, when you hang yourself you have

54

to do it right, a quick snapping action as you reach the bottom of the rope and the neck breaks, but if not, you will hang there and choke to death, it is very unpleasant and painful" the dummy informed him.

"Please, let me go" the agent managed to say eventually.

"Did Cynthia say them words to you while you raped her, got her so drunk she didn't know what the hell was happening, did you slap her about a bit just for the fun of it"

Geoff asked him as he wobbled precariously on the chair.

"He is not looking very well Geoff" the dummy said turning its head to look at Geoff then spinning round back to the agent again.

"My sister never recovered from what you did to her, too shy, too scared to tell anyone she became a shell, empty, a shadow of her bubbly joyful self. You took her life and her dreams from her. Used her for your own gratification and sexual pleasure, well today she is going to be revenged, today you are going to die and a painful death at that" Geoff told him while he watched him slip and wobble on the chair. The rope was tight and felt threatening and he was scared, the whiskey had made him unstable and he began to wet himself again.

"You are fucking disgusting do you know that" the dummy said shaking its head.

"You've not even said sorry, never asked about her, never shown any remorse or regret, all you have done is offered me money and pleaded for yourself, you selfish bastard" Geoff said as he watched him cry and stagger to one side, the rope tightening on his neck.

He reached up and tried to untie it, he was desperate and struggled to undo the rope, he lost balance and slipped to one side the chair followed and it leaned over on two legs. A cry of terror and fear came from him as his weight shifted and he miss footed the chair completely. It fell over and he dropped the rope tight round his neck strangling him, he choked and reached up trying to take his weight but he was too drunk and had no coordination or strength to do so. He began to kick out as his throat burned and the pain tore into his neck, he was gasping for air as the rope choked him. His whole body swung violently catching sight of the dummy laughing at him as he turned round and started to lose consciousness. The air supply was cut off as he frantically reached and grabbed for the rope but it was no good, he was choking. His tongue was swelling and filling his mouth, his eyes bulged in their sockets with the pressure.

Geoff watched until he was still, his body turning on the rope round his neck, his body limp, the life choked from him.

Geoff looked at the dummy and the dummy looked at him saying

"It was too good for him. It should have taken longer"

"Well at least, he will not be abusing anyone else will he" Geoff answered.

"We should be on the stage you and me; we would bring the house down"

Geoff didn't say anything as he walked from the room and then the house, unseen and unnoticed. The body was left hanging there slowly turning and swaying, he looked hideous and smelt terrible, but then again people were always used to him being disgusting.

The End

# POPPY SELLER

She must have been at least eighty-five years old, frail and weak looking, sat on a small wooden chair behind a small table, at the Shopping Arcade entrance. The table had a plastic money box on it and a neatly set out line of pin-on poppy badges and artificial flowers. It was Remembrance Day and she was selling the red poppy flower as a mark of respect and honour, and to raise money for the appeal that helped the soldiers and families of the Armed Forces, past and present. She was wrapped up and had a shawl over her shoulders, most people were ignoring her and just walking past, some young teenager girls sniggered and giggled at her as they passed by. The older generation stopped, smiled and put some coins in her plastic box and were rewarded for their kindness with a pin on poppy and a smile back.

Watching this from across the way in a small cafe was Keith. He was about fifty years old and was disgusted at what he was witnessing. Most people just ignored the poor woman and she got nasty looks and some horrible sniggers from younger girls but she stayed there and carried on doing her bit for the cause.

"More tea love" a voice said which made him look round.

A waitress was looking at him and his empty cup.

"Err yes please and one of them cream slices under the counter there" he said with a smile.

"Sad isn't it, the old lass there" she said nodding over to where the old woman was sat.

"It makes me sick, I have been watching and most people just walking by not even looking at her, some taking the piss and I feel like going over and saying what an ungrateful bunch of bastards you all are, here she is collecting for war veterans which is what she probably is or her family at least, and they can't even make a donation, God knows what the poor lass and her family went through. We just don't know what she has done in the war, for Christ sake they deserve much better than this, why don't they leave someone with her?"

"I agree but that is what they are like these days, no bloody respect and no bloody manners, you should hear the language and abuse we get in here sometimes from school kids, in my day you got a clip round the ear hole for talking like that"

"That is what they are short of these days, a bloody good hiding and some discipline, I would never dream of disrespecting my elders when I was younger"

"You can't touch your kids now, they know it and they just take the piss" she walked away and got him his cream slice and tea, he turned and looked out of the window then stood up saying out to her across the cafe

"Won't be a minute love" he went out and walked over to the old lady selling her poppies. Taking a ten pound note from his wallet he folded it and slipped it in her collection box, she smiled and a very quiet and frail voice thanked him. He took his poppy and wore it with pride thanking her for her efforts and what she was doing, shook her hand then asked if she would like a coffee or anything bringing over, her face lit up as she nodded. Reaching for some money from her purse she was going to pay him but he stopped her and smiled. Dashing back he ordered her a coffee and a cream bun and when they were ready he ran back over with them. She smiled and thanked him warmly.

"It is the least we can do, if it wasn't for you and people like you we would not be here, I cannot thank you all enough" he shook her hand once more and smiled, he then went back to the cafe and sat with his cream slice and tea.

The waitress came over and cleaned the table next to him with a cloth she smiled and said.

"You will be rewarded in heaven"

"I just cannot understand why people do not appreciate the sacrifice that has been made for them, why the hell are people walking past her and ignoring her, a few bloody bob in a plastic box is not much to ask is it, for fuck sake what is this world coming to?"

"It's no good getting high rate about it that is the way it is these days"

62

"It's so wrong; a nation that forgets its past has no future"

"Nicely put and so true" she nodded her head in agreement and went back to serve some customers that had just came in.

He took a sip of his tea and finishing his cream slice, he knew he had to go, but somehow felt sad about leaving the old girl across the road. He said his goodbye to the waitress and left taking one more look across at the old girl then went on his way.

The day had been a long one for the poppy seller, she had been there now for several hours and she was feeling tired and exhausted. She looked at the small watch on her thin frail wrist and saw she had at least two more hours before they were going to come and pick her up.

They normally send someone to check every hour but today they were very short staffed and she had not seen anyone. Her table was roughly knocked by some people walking past, they paid it no attention and just carried on, she struggled to pull it back straight and rearrange the small display she had on it. Finishing her coffee and cake she put the cup down on the floor by her side. Then took a deep breath and sighed, she moved and stretched her leg out, the arthritis was painful, moving it hurt her but staying in one position hurt as well. She repositioned on the chair and got as comfortable as she could. A young woman dropped some coins in her collection box but didn't stop or say anything as she walked on by. She watched her walk away and said nothing keeping her thoughts to herself.

Then she noticed a man, scruffy dressed and dark skinned, he was stood across from her staring, it made her feel a bit uneasy. He was an evil looking man and his eyes were cold. Only about twenty years old, unshaven and with a nasty expression on his face, he looked at her and did not hide the fact that he was doing so.

She looked away and did not make eye contact, she suddenly felt very vulnerable and scared, and there was no one to help her, no one to see the fear in her eyes. Looking down at her table she focused on the little red flowers she was selling and tried to put him out of her mind, hoping he would go away.

She could not help but glance up every now and then in the hope he would be gone but he was not, he was still looking at her, you could call it hate that was in his eyes. She did not know what to do, she could not run or even leave, she was stuck and becoming very nervous and anxious with the situation. She noticed her hands were shaking and her breathing had become more heavy and irregular. He knew he was stressing her out and he seemed to enjoy it, in some sick cowardice way he enjoyed the power of fear he had over the helpless and defenceless old lady. He smiled a dirty smile and started to stare at her with widened eyes as she glanced up at him from time to time. She no longer noticed the odd person dropping a few pennies into her tin. She just wanted to be away and be safe. Then she noticed the lady from the cafe walking over to her, she sighed a sigh of anticipated relief and put her hands out to greet her as she came over.

"Just come across to make sure you are alright love do you want another coffee?" she asked with a smile, but changed her expression when she saw the fear and panic on the old ladies face.

"Can I please come to your cafe, that man is scaring me" she had dread and panic in her voice and tears in her eyes. The waitress looked over and saw the man smiling at her, she instantly disliked him and made sure her facial expression told him so.

"Yes of course you can, come on let's get you packed up and you can come over and stay in there until he has gone and we can get someone to come and pick you up"

She placed all the tables contents in a bag that was under it then folded the table up, and also the chair she was sat on. Struggling she got these under her arm and in her right hand while she helped the old lady with her left. They slowly made their way to the cafe and she sat her down. The man watched and sniggered and then came to the window looking in at them.

"Take no notice darling he is just a prat, I will get you a nice coffee" the waitress made the lady face into the cafe so she could not see him at the window, she got her a coffee and came and sat down with her for a short time while the place was quiet.

"Thank you; I will pay you for the coffee, how much is it?" the lady asked.

"It's on the house darling, you have done enough and deserve to be waited on and respected."

"That man scared me, he would not stop looking at me in that way, I don't think I have offended him I am very sorry if I have" her voice was full of worry and it made the waitress sad to see and hear it.

"You have done nothing wrong, he is just an idiot and will go away soon, when is somebody coming to collect you, surely they should not just leave you alone like this?"

"Not normally, but today they seem to have forgotten me" she smiled a timid smile and took a slow sip of her coffee holding the mug in both hands.

"Have you a number I can ring or someone I can call to come and collect you?"

She shook her head and just smiled; the waitress looked out of the window and saw the man sticking his tongue out at them and then laughing. She looked past him and saw Keith walking back the way he had gone earlier. She stood and went to the door; she got his attention and waved him over, the man at the window backed away when he saw Keith coming towards them. The waitress explained the situation and when Keith went to confront the man he hurried away. They both came back into the cafe and Keith went to sit with the old lady. She smiled at him and he smiled back at her as he sat down opposite her.

"You alright sexy?" he smiled.

"Oh it's a long time since I was called that young man"

"Well it's a long time since I was called a young man"

"You know I knew many young men, when I was younger, my father was only a young man when he went to war, they say it's the Great War but there is nothing great about it. It was terrible what it did to him and all the brave men who marched off to France and fought in that terrible time, dug into trenches, it was horrendous and hell on earth, the stench, the sight of body parts being blown to pieces, the bodies you had buried being blown up again with each

68

explosion, the rats, the lice, the disease. The freezing cold, and frost bite, the shell shock of your comrades and friends, the torturous insanity of it all, they were never the same again when they had been there; it was not humane to put men through that. It was sickening to think they had to put up with. Being ordered to go over the top knowing it meant being shot and killed. The bravery of the soldiers and the stupidity of the generals"

"That is what the Germans said in the second world war, the English Soldiers are lions led by donkeys" Keith put out his hand and placed it on top of hers, he could see the horrible memories flooding back to her as she thought about her father. He felt sorry for her, all she had been through all she must have suffered and she is still here collecting for the Remembrance Day, and fallen soldiers past and present. It humbled him and he felt proud to be able to sit with her.

"You are a nice man and it is nice people like you and the lady that make it all worthwhile, but I do not understand the young people these days, so much hate, nastiness, greed, selfishness and

69

lazy I just cannot understand it" she slowly shook her head and bowed it to the table.

"Society is too free and easy nowadays, what is your name by the way?"

"My name is Grace, Grace Taylor"

"Keith, pleased to meet you Grace" he smiled and shook her hand; she smiled back then glanced out of the window and was relieved to see the man was gone.

"Don't worry no one will harm you, I will make sure you get home safe today" he said with a smile. She smiled back at him then just stared into his eyes; she was still and silent for a moment and seemed to be reading into him. She eventually took his hand and he felt how brittle and weak her hand was.

"Keith you are a good man, I can see into your soul, I have met many people in my life some good and many bad, I have heard horrific stories of the wars and the terrible things people do to each other. I cannot understand the hate and greed of this world, the sacrifice and pain people endured to keep this land safe and free, it

70

seems sometimes that it has all been in vain and wasted but when I see people who are honest and kind then these people make it all worthwhile. I just do not know what is going to happen in this world and sometimes I am glad I will not be around to see it, but I feel sorry for the good people and nice people who will have to endure it" she smiled and squeezed his hand.

"You have many years left yet Grace"

She smiled and shook her head saying to him in a soft voice.

"No my new friend I do not, my husband died many years ago, I miss him terribly and soon will be back with him. My son was killed fighting the terrorists in Northern Ireland"

"My God Grace your father was in the first World War, your son killed by the bloody IRA and you are such a wonderful woman full of kindness and compassion, why can't there be more people like you in the world"

"Its people like you we need Keith, good honest people with morals and respect"

The waitress came back over after serving a customer and sat down smiling at them both.

"Hello again" Keith said with a smile.

"Hello, how are we, do either of you need anything?" Grace took her hand and held it tight she looked her in the eye and smiled at her before saying softly.

"No thank you love, I will be going now it is almost my time, but you are a good girl and you two should get together some time it will be good for both of you"

She slightly blushed and looked at Keith who was smiling back at her, then looked back at Grace and asked.

"Can I give you a lift home Grace, it is the least I can do"

"You can give me a lift Keith yes, I do not live too far from here really, that would be nice, maybe you can come too" she said looking at the waitress.

"Well I do get off in about ten minutes actually and a lift home would be great my feet are killing me"

"I don't mind there is plenty of room in my car, and it's not every day I get two beautiful woman to drive about with is it."

"Oh you are a smooth talker Keith, Grace said with a smile.

It was only a matter of twenty minutes later when he was driving them home, Grace was sat in the front seat and the waitress in the back of the car, she was pleased of the lift and very grateful, the long walk home after being on her feet all day was a killer to her sometimes. Grace gave the directions and Keith gladly followed, it was a nursing home that she lived at, leaning back into her seat she turned and asked the waitress.

"What is your name my dear?"

"Jill, Jillian," she answered with a smile.

"Well it has been a pleasure to meet you Jillian and you too Keith" she said turning to him.

"The pleasure as been all mine Grace, you are a wonderful and very remarkable woman"

"Yes you are Grace and I am very pleased to have met you too" Jillian added.

"Thank you both, it is always nice to make new friends." She opened the door and started to get out, Geoff opened his door and ran round to help her, he carried her table and things in for her and walked her into the building, and she turned and waved at Jillian before she went in. Moments later Keith came back out and got into the car.

"What a fantastic woman, so much can be learned from a person like that" he said looking straight out of the window and had a look of awe on his face.

"Yes she is a remarkable lady, I pass this place when I walk to work, and all this time I have just walked past and not known she lives here"

"I hope to meet her again, one day"

"I might pop in tomorrow just to see how she is, that wanker today really scared her, what a bloody tosser"

"I should have ran after the twat and gave him an hiding"

"I just hate the way he made her feel and he knew exactly what he was doing, why do people do such horrible things, what pleasure do they get out of it?"

"Makes you sick what this world has come to" Keith shook his head then pulled away back onto the main road, Jillian gave him directions and minutes later he slowly stopped outside her flat. He looked back and smiled at her.

"Thank you very much Keith that has been a great help"

"No problem" he said with a smile.

"Will you be in the cafe tomorrow I could buy you a cream slice and a tea as a thank you?"

"I will pop in if I get time yes thank you"

"OK, no problem" she smiled and got out of the car and Keith watched her walk to her flat. He sensed she was expecting a little more and maybe an invite to a date but he said nothing, he didn't know why. The next day he did manage to get to the cafe and he knew something was wrong as soon as he walked in, Jill was looking worried and upset, and she came straight up to him as he walked through to a table.

"Keith, she died last night, Grace passed away in her sleep, I popped in this morning to see her and they told me" she had tears in her eyes and welcomed the hug Keith gave her. They were silent for a moment then they both sat down at a table. Instinctively they both stared over to where she had been sat the day before. No one cared and just went on with their lives; Keith slowly shook his head with sadness, and then looked at Jill, who had tears in her eyes.

"Do you fancy going for a drink tonight in the memory of a remarkable and wonderful woman we both knew for a short time but will never forget?"

"Would love too"

It was around seven when he picked her up, she looked very beautiful in a trouser suit and he smiled to himself as she walked to the car and got in.

"Good evening pretty lady" he said with a smile.

"Good evening kind gent" she replied with the same smile.

76

They had a night that was pleasing and comforting for them both, after a few drinks Keith drove them to a restaurant and they had a meal, they talked about each other and the conversation was flowing and came easy, they discovered they had a lot in common and got on very well. As they were walking back to the car they talked about Grace and what a remarkable lady she must have been. Keith unlocked his car and they both got in, and instantly froze, they both looked at it, the car had been locked and no one could have got in, it was not there when they left the car earlier. A single poppy was placed on the dash board. A single poppy flower put there for them both to see. They slowly looked at each other and both seemed to know what the other one was thinking. Together they smiled and without shame or feeling foolish they smiled again. They looked at the poppy for a few moments and both simultaneously said

"Grace"

The End

# I SEE GHOSTS

It had been such a long night, he didn't like working the night shift especially at the weekend, but he needed the money as he just bought this new car and it now had to pay it off. Saturday night was always the worst, drunks, noisy annoying young girls, people running off without paying, some even sick in the back of the car. He didn't like Saturday nights but tonight had not been too bad, one more fare and he was heading home. He turned into the street and saw her. She looked so out of place but only because it was Saturday night and she was dressed sensible and conservative like. She patiently waited by the side of the road and he pulled up. She got into the back and politely gave him her address. He noticed her looking out onto the front of his car for a moment then settled back into her seat. He glanced in his mirror and then pulled off away and on his last customer then he could go home. He drove steady and then had to break hard. Someone had just run out in front of him shouting obscenities at him and then staggered off.

"I am sorry" he apologised looking at her in his mirror and carried on

"No problem, its Saturday night what do you expect" her voice was warm and educated, he liked it instantly. It was such a nice change to have someone who can actually talk like an intelligent person in his car, especially on a Saturday night at this time.

"Yeah it can get a bit crazy, you wouldn't believe what I have to put up with some nights, and this town is getting worse" he said back to her in an equally friendly voice.

"I can imagine, how long have you had this car if you don't mind me asking?"

"I have just got it only a few days?" he was a little puzzled how she seemed to know.

"Oh okay that's fine" she said looking out onto his bonnet again.

"What made you say that?" he asked puzzled.

"I will tell you when I am home don't worry about it" she smiled at him and settled back into her seat. He drove the rest of the way in silence and was soon at her address. He pulled up and she opened her purse and asked him how much.

"That is just six pounds twenty thanks"

"Thank you, keep the change" she gave him a ten pound note and opened the door to leave.

"How did you know about the car being bought recently?" he asked her.

She sighed and looked at him then out onto his bonnet again, then back at him.

"You have a spirit, ghost on this car, he is on your bonnet right now" she said soberly and without any emotion or expression.

"What, what the hell you talking about?" he said looking onto his bonnet and seeing nothing.

"He is looking straight at you, was doing all the way you drove here, this car has killed, I do not know what he wants but he is not happy" she said looking out onto his bonnet again.

"Don't talk so bloody stupid, there is no one there, look" he pointed and gave a nervous laugh shaking his head in disbelief.

"You will not get rid of him, not until you find out what he is angry about or what he wants, if you have mirrors in your house you might start seeing shadows in them, it is how they try to communicate, depends how receptive you are or if you are willing to be open"

"Yeah ok, long night I know, I have to get home now thanks" he said looking away from her with a scoff and shake of his head.

She said no more and got out of the car and walked up a small drive and into a small house. He for some reason didn't really know why, made a mental note of where she lived then remembered the address.

Driving home he kept looking on his bonnet, there was nothing there, nothing on it just an empty bonnet. He got home and parked up. It was late and he was tired. He locked his car and looked at it for a moment. He then tentatively touched the bonnet. It was warm the car had been running all night so that was normal. He waved his hand across it in front of the driver's side windscreen.

He shook his head feeling stupid and looked around seeing if anyone was watching him. Going into his house he closed the door and went up to bed, while he was brushing his teeth he looked into the mirror. Looking at his reflection then the reflection of his surroundings, he laughed to himself and shook his head. He went to bed but left the light on all night.

Sunday was a rainy day and he planned on staying in all day and doing nothing. It was his recharge time. He could not get out of his mind what the woman had said to him. She seemed genuine enough not some delusional idiot or anything. He thought about it while he made breakfast and then had a shower after. He got out of the shower cubical in his bathroom; the steam from the hot water was everywhere, he had to open a window to get rid of it normally. He stopped and stared at the mirror on his wall, it was clear, no steam on it, no condensation at all. It was totally clear. The rest of the room was not and he slowly reached out and opened the bathroom window. He looked at the mirror and could not understand why it was clear as normally it was frosted up with condensation when he took a shower. He got dried and didn't look at it again as he walked out into his bedroom and got dressed. But curiosity got the better of him. He slowly and nervously looked back into the bathroom. The place was clearing now the window was open. He looked over at the mirror and saw it had some condensation on it. He sighed and smiled to himself and thought he was being stupid.

He dismissed it and spent the rest of the day doing nothing, he liked the solitude of being alone sometimes and it recharged his inner strength and mind. The night came in fast and he switched just his side light on and watched a bit of TV. When he was due to go to bed he happened to look at his living room door and the gap at the bottom let light through from his hallway. He was not sure but he thought he saw a shadow, something block the light, was it someone walking past the door?

He was startled and stood up quickly. He went to the door and with his heart racing he opened it fast. He looked about but there was no one there. He went and checked his front door, it was still locked. He went to the back door, this also was locked. He looked round and could see or hear nothing. He put it down to him being tired and went up to bed. He turned all the lights out and went into the bathroom. He brushed his teeth and avoided looking in the mirror then got into bed, leaving the light on once again. He tried to sleep but could not. He was spooked and thought he heard noises then pulled his feet in close and didn't dare hang them over the side. Eventually he fell into a troubled sleep but was awakened in the early hours of the morning. By what he didn't know, he looked up and focused his eyes to the room, all seemed well. The light was still on and it was quiet. He yawned and needed to go to the toilet; he got out of bed and headed that way. What he didn't see was the shadow on the wall behind him following him as he went. A shadow but there was no one else in the room, a shadow but the light was on and not causing a shadow. He lifted the seat up and urinated. He then came back out of the bathroom and got the shock of his life, he caught sight of it in the mirror as he walked past. He screamed in fear and froze momentarily. A face looking at him, a

84

man's face, there in the mirror staring at him, eyes fixed on his. Looking out from the mirror as if he was on the other side of a window, backing up he dashed from the bathroom and grabbed his clothes and hurried downstairs, he was petrified. He raced for the door and grabbed his keys, he ran from the house and in a panic he got into his car. He was shaking and scared like he had never been scared before in his entire life. He drove away not knowing where just away from his house. He turned the rear view mirror up so he could not see it. He was still shaking and shook his head trying to think straight. He slowed down and then stopped by the side of the road. He breathed heavy and his heart was racing in his chest. He calmed himself and thought about it all for a moment, was he dreaming? Was he still half awake? What did he actually see was it his own reflection and his mind playing games on him? All these questions went through his head. He turned the mirror back down and looked through it, all seemed ok, and he looked out to the bonnet of his car but obviously could see nothing. He took a deep breath and sighed out not knowing what to think. He waited until later that morning, he dare not go home. He went round to the woman's house. She said she saw something and he wanted to know what it was. He parked up outside her little house and turned off his engine, he felt foolish and stupid and dare not go ask her. He was there for several minutes when the front door opened and the woman came out, she walked straight up to his car and knocked on the side window.

He smiled and wound it down, she looked at him and stared into his eyes for a moment before she spoke.

"You have seen him then, he made contact, he is not on your car at this moment so where is he?" she asked him and was serious and sober.

"Well I don't know what to say, I am sorry for coming round but things have happened and I feel bloody stupid really, I am sorry for coming round" he was embarrassed and was not sure how to approach what he wanted to say or even how to say it.

"It is alright I told you he was there, he was shouting at you, but he is gone from your car now, he will be back though, he will never be able to be disjointed from this vehicle I don't think, I would say it has killed and something is very wrong" she didn't falter when she was saying these things and they were just as natural and ordinary to her as any conversation.

"The car is fine it has not killed anyone?" he said confused.

"How do you know, where did you get it from?"

"Dealership, it was a part exchange they told me and they did a background check, it has not been in any kind of accident"

"And you believe them, have you checked to see if it has been repaired at all?"

"Well no, but they have to tell you don't they" he was beginning to sound and feel stupid and wished he had not come.

She smiled and told him to wait there she went back into the house and came back with a small but powerful square magnet. He got out and she stood by the back of the car, she placed the magnet on the paint work and it stuck to the car. He watched her go round the vehicle and did the same thing as she did. She came to the front driver's side and the magnet would not stick onto the front wing area, she looked at him and pointed to it.

"What am I looking at?" he asked a little confused.

"The magnet holds onto metal, it won't stick there, so it is not metal it is body filler, the car has been repaired, sprayed over and you will never know" she sighed out and looked at him seeing his deflated and worried look she decided to help him.

"The lying bastards, they told me it had not and even checked it for me" he told her.

"Well like I said these things are not always reported are they, do you know who the last owner was, or is it down as the dealership?"

"Dealership they had the car for a while I believe I got a great deal on it actually"

"You know why now, don't you?"

"What can I do, can you help me can you come and exorcise it" he regretted saying it as soon as it came out of his mouth. She shook her head and laughed out slightly.

"No, I cannot do these things I can just see them, hear them, they know who can see them and communicate through these people sometimes, other times they don't, they just are visible and do nothing, but also sometimes they make people like you see them, it wants something or needs something from you. It was very angry and shouting at you when I saw it the other night in your car"

"What can I do, what should I do, I dare not go back to the house" he was genuinely worried and although he must have looked and sounded like a coward, she didn't judge him.

"Find out what it wants, then it will go away, go to rest" she told him calmly.

"That's easy for you to say, it is in my house, I saw its shadow under my door then a face in the mirror, what the hell can I do, I am shitting myself here" he shook his head and took a deep exaggerated breath.

"You will be surprised what I have seen and heard, you have no idea. I did not ask for this, I just have the gift or whatever you want to call it where I can see them. I wake up at night sometimes

89

and my room is full of people, spirits, I have seen dead bodies floating across the room, you have no idea what I have to see and live with. And you see one face in a fucking mirror and you collapse into hysteria?" her tone changed and he felt the resentment and annoyance in her voice and regretted what he had said.

"I am sorry, it is just all new to me, I have never experienced anything like this before. I know it must be terrible for you, please forgive my ignorance" he genuinely said to her.

"All you can do is go home and ask it what it wants from you, ask for a sign anything, it might even be able to communicate with you and talk to you. Man up and go ask it" she smiled at him and backed off and he could see she wanted to get back into her house.

"Ok, well thank you for your help, I am sorry again for disturbing you and coming round like a bloody idiot." he smiled and felt stupid. She smiled back at him politely and then walked back into her house. He wanted to ask her to come and talk to it but he dare not. He got back into his car and drove over to the dealership where he bought the car from, he was met with hostility and don't want to know attitude. They even accused him of doing the repair himself. He had no luck there and knew they were not reputable so would be fighting a losing battle. He asked for the previous owner but again got nothing.

He stayed out most of the morning but knew he had to go back. He plucked up enough courage and went back that afternoon. He parked up and looked at his front door for a few minutes before slowly getting out of his car. He took a deep breath and went in, he had to be brave and face this he knew that now, he had felt foolish the way he acted earlier to that woman. He closed the door behind him, all seemed quiet and all seemed normal. He went into the living room and looked around then clenched his fists and gritted his teeth. Going up to the bathroom he felt his heart pound in his rib cage. He went into the bathroom and looked into the mirror. All he saw was his reflection looking back. He was unshaven and looked drained, he was tired and felt stupid for what he was about to do, but he did it anyway.

"Who are you and what do you want?" he said in a low voice, and then he said it again in a louder voice. He was just looking back at himself in the mirror and nothing happened. The rest of the day was uneventful and he began to think it was all in his mind. He had to work that night and got on early. Monday nights was not too bad and normally quiet. He got his usual mixture of fares. Then a feminine man got into his car, he was late twenties and looked what he was, gay, he seemed rushed and didn't look at the car or the driver, he just hurried and got in quickly.

"Where to buddy?" he asked his passenger.

"Oh, take me to Oxford Street" his voice was sharp and to the point of being rude.

As he drove he glanced in his mirror and saw his passenger looking around the inside of the car and getting a little agitated.

"You alright?" he asked looking in his rear view mirror, seeing this gay man looking puzzled.

"Yes just drive, just drive and hurry up" he snapped back at him.

Suddenly the car jolted and missed, the mirror misted over and then cleared again, the wheel began to vibrate and all the doors locked. The passenger became agitated and looked around confused and scared.

The car seemed to be driving itself even though he was pressing the foot pedals, nothing was happening. The engine over revved and the car just took over like it had a mind of its own. It drove fast and out up near the lake. The passenger began to scream and demand he stop, pulling at the door handles as he tried to get out. He then screamed and shook uncontrollably throwing himself back into the back seats, shaking like a leaf. He pointed to the rear view mirror. It had cleared and the face was there glaring back at his passenger. The car was not under his control and he could do nothing. Screaming they both tried to get out but all doors were locked. Suddenly the car stopped just on the edge of the lake. Next to a large tree, the driver's door opened and without a second hesitation he dived out, the door slammed shut behind him. He looked into the car and saw his passenger screaming with terror and shouting to the face in the mirror. Running towards the lake he stopped then looked back as another scream came from the car then all was quiet. He eventually went back to the car and peered in, his passenger was just sat on the back seat staring forward and saying nothing. Trying the doors he found they were locked and he could not get in. Eventually he rang the police he didn't know what else to do.

It was a whole week later he was knocking on the door of the woman who had told him about the man on the bonnet of his car. He waited and eventually she answered.

He just went round to tell her what had happened and how the passenger admitted to killing his lover, running him over in that car, she was right it had been damaged where he rammed into him. The car was sold last year and somehow had found its way back to this town even though it had been sold over two hundred miles away. The passenger admitted everything to the police, he was petrified and the police had asked what he had done to him. He then told them his whole story which they found hard to believe, but they had solved a murder and had a confession so they were happy in any case. She was happy for him and he left, he never saw her again. He sold the car and to this day he has no mirrors in his house.


The End

# The Stranger

She didn't like driving alone, she felt uncomfortable with it, her ex husband told her it was insecurity, he told her a lot of things, mostly insulting and degrading. She had put up with it and tolerated it for many years but when she finally found the message on his phone she snapped. She had suspicions beforehand but she chose to ignore them. There comes a time when you just cannot ignore and bury your head in the sand anymore. He was having an affair and that was the end.

She shook her head and dislodged the thought and the memories that would always follow.

She took a deep breath and looked out into the night ahead, the lights illuminating the way along the quiet road.

She noticed the light come on next to the fuel gauge. Looking at it she frowned for a moment until it registered what it meant. She felt a surge of panic rise in her stomach and she looked round inside the car but for what she didn't know. She peered for a moment at her fuel gauge, it had reached the red line, and she was not sure how much fuel she had left. Never letting her tank get this empty before, she looked up and back out of her windscreen at the dark road ahead of her.

Unconsciously she slowed down in some attempt to save petrol. She was breathing heavily and a hint of the panic returned. Swallowing because her throat had become dry she looked worried and scared. Never a strong person and always a little vulnerable she gripped the wheel tight as she desperately looked for some sign that would help her into a town or petrol station.

Always glancing down at the light on her dash board, always following that with a look at her fuel gauge, she didn't know how long she was driving but the sign on the side on the road made her smile, then laugh with relief.

"Thank God" she said out loud to herself as she pulled off the road and followed the signs that led her to the small petrol station situated off the main road.

She smiled to herself as she pulled up next to the pump and

turned off her engine.

She noticed him walking across in front of her car and into the shop where you pay, glancing round she could see no other cars and wondered where he had came from.

She got out and to a deep welcoming breath of crisp night air, stretching she arched her back and breathed out.

After filling the car to the hilt, she screwed the cap back on and closed the small flap to hide it from view. Reaching in she got her purse from her bag and went to pay.

He was stood by the door just on the inside and smiled at her as she walked past, she nodded and smiled back. Walking to the desk she paid and turned to leave, he was gone, but she noticed him again out on the forecourt.

Walking to her car, he approached her and smiled a very friendly smile, saying in an equally friendly voice.

"Hello, I am so sorry to bother you but is there any chance you could help me please?"

"I'm not sure and really in a hurry" she said not stopping as
98

she walked to her car.

His face showed discouraging sag and he forced a smile before saying in a disappointing voice.

"Sorry for bothering you"

She walked to her car and looked back to see him still standing and looking lost, her instinct took the better of her and she shouted from her car as she opened the door.

"Are you in some sort of trouble?"

"My wife and child are in the car down the road and we ran out of petrol, I have come here to get some, but they don't have a petrol can would you believe?"

"I do not carry one either, I am sorry" She got back into her car and started the engine.

She watched as he walked away and headed off down the road into the darkness, she pulled off slowly and drove out onto the same road.

He looked very nice and he looked very honest, but she could never trust a man again and the hurt and pain was still there.

She caught sight of him in her head lights just as the rain came down. It started slow but within moments it was steady, she put her wipers on and watched as he curled up with his hands in his pockets and put his head down as he walked.

Not knowing why, she found herself pulling up along side of him and taking the window down she shouted across to him.

"How far is it you have to go?"

He stopped and came to the car window, he popped his head half way in and she noticed his big pleasing blue eyes look at her.

"About a mile I suppose maybe a little more, not too far" he said with a charming smile.

"I can give you a lift if it is only a mile or two"

Thank you so very much" He smiled and quickly got into the car closing the door after him and giving a little shiver as he sat in the warmth again.

The window went up and she pulled off slowly into the night watching the road and a little worried at what she had done.

"You are a very nice lady thank you; the garage owner was not helpful at all"

"I cannot believe they would not lend you any kind of petrol can?"

"Well they say it is not something they do, and were not very nice to be honest"

"So what are you going to do?"

"What do you mean?" he said looking across at her.

"About your wife and child"

"My wife?" he said with a frown.

"Yes, you said your wife and child are in a car up the road?"

"Did I, no, I ate my wife some time ago"

She felt a dread and an empty pit in her stomach as she looked over at him looking at her, his face was serious and didn't look friendly any more.

"What did you say?" she slowed and stopped the car, fear reaching up inside her and making her nervous.

"I ate her in a stew with carrots, spuds and a bit of parsnip, she tasted like pork, they always said it would and they were right, human flesh tastes like pork"

"Get out, get out now" she shouted at him as confident and as sternly as she could.

He reached into his pocket and pulled out a grenade, he clasped it in his right hand and pulled the pin with his left, without warning he put his hand under her skirt and rested the cold metal of the grenade against her knickers and crotch.

She gasped with fear and her eyes widened, she tried to say something and rise off the seat away from his hand between her legs, but she could not.

"This has a very short fuse, it will explode long before you can get out of this car, killing us both, I am not afraid of death, it is my friend" he said calmly while looking out of the front window at the rain falling.

"What do you want, please, please, just let me go" she muttered through the tears that were streaming from her eyes and down her face. She could not move and shook uncontrollably.

"Do as you are told, drive and we will have a nice chat." he looked at her and she noticed his eyes had become cold and staring. She shook and just cried with fear and torment, she could do nothing else and she felt the fear grip her like a vice.

"Please, just take that away, please I will... just take it away ....."

"I have dropped the pin, and do not know where it is, now drive along and we will have a chat then you can go home, can't you?"

"I can't, I can't drive with that there please move it" she pleaded through her tears.

"Fucking drive you whore" he shouted with a powerful volume that made her jump with terror and cry out with fear.

"Please, "she sobbed at him.

"Drive, drive or I will blow you to fuck, now get going bitch" he looked at her with a fire of hate in his eyes.

She reluctantly started to drive off but she stalled the car and it halted with a judder, she panicked with anxiety and fear. The whole uncomfortable situation was too straining for her.

He stared at her and she turned away, somehow feeling if she didn't look at him the situation would be easier. She managed to start the car and ease it off again driving slowly down the road and crying as she did. His hand moved and she jumped as he repositioned the grenade next to her inner thigh and knickers.

"Do not piss yourself either, I do not want all that over my hand do you understand?"

"Please….." she said but jumped and was quiet as he shouted back violently and angrily at her as soon as she spoke.

"Stop fucking saying that word, fucking please, please, please" he mocked.

"What do you want?" she shouted through her fear.

"To talk to you, for you to drive and stop being a weak pathetic fuck, do you think you can do that, do you think you can do anything?"

"To talk?" she said not taking her eyes of the road ahead she dare not look at him and concentrated on driving in the rain and dark.

"They fall for it every time, nice eyes they say, lovely smile they say, charming they say,

I am not who they think I am, I am not who anybody thinks I am."

"Where am I driving to?" She tried to calm herself and felt if she kept him talking he was calmer and less volatile.

"What is your name, you just keep going if you go wrong I will tell you and you can correct your route, what is your name?"

"Harriet" she said still not looking at him.

"I will never know if that is your real name or you are lying to me, I could of course search your bag or purse to make sure but I am not that bothered really to be honest"

He must be unstable and dangerous she thought, he was volatile and she knew nothing of how to handle this situation, but she had a survival instinct and knew she must get somewhere where there was someone who could help her, she tried hard to calm herself and drive carefully. Having a grenade in your crotch was not the most ideal situation to be in, let alone having a mad man holding it with the pin released.

"What does it feel like having a strangers hand on your pussy holding a live grenade, what is going through your head, is it a turn on Harriet?" he asked her serenely.

Breathy heavy and desperately trying to calm her nerves, she attempted to have a conversation with this maniac in her car.

"It feels very threatening and frightening"

"Not kinky then, not exciting, not a turn on at all?" he said.

"No, not at all maybe there is no need for it to be there, I can still drive you anywhere you want to go" she said hopefully.

He smiled and then laughed a long laugh out loud, his hand shook against her knickers and she flinched and tried to calm herself and drive at the same time.

"Do not even try to play games with me Harriet or whatever your fucking name is. I have had many psychotherapists, analysts and doctors talk to me. Did you know most psychotherapist are more fucked in the head then the people they are trying to help, they have these vulnerable and weak people come to them or sent to them and they just impose their fears and demons onto them and make them believe something that has not even happened or does not even exist. Did you know most of them are more troubled, more fucked up, more twisted then their patients?"

"I don't know" she shook her head, not knowing how answer his question.

"Well it is true, they are all fucking mental, fucked up, twisted, evil, psychotic bitches believe me, I fucking know, they should not be let loose on the victims they call patients."

"Where are we going, please just tell me what you want from me?"

"Keep driving and avoid cities and towns, I want quiet roads. Take me home to your house so we can have a nice cup of tea" he smiled at her and patted her on the knee with his left hand gently making her flinch.

"I live too far away from here; I don't live anywhere close at all?"

"I could look in your bag and find out if you are lying to me, but I cannot be fucking bothered Harriet or whatever your fucking name is, keep driving and if I see any cities, towns or people I will blow us both to hell, I am a welcome visitor there and know it well so it is up to you Harriet, or whatever your fucking name is"

"I will try my best to stay clear then" she said in her most calming voice she could muster in this situation she found herself.

"That's better, that is more like it, now where were we, I tell you what, why don't you tell me something about yourself?"

"What like, there is nothing to tell" she said nervously.

"Where do you live, what do you like, where have you been, what is your pain tolerance and what is your most disgusting habit, lots of things?"

"I live near London." she started but was abruptly stopped as he shouted once again at her with a venomous screech.

"NO, no, no, we are a long way from London which is why you have said that, I am not stupid, I am many things but not stupid, it is you who is stupid my dear, now let's start again, what is your most inner fear?"

"I don't know," she shook her head.

"You do, or maybe you don't yet, because if you have not experienced true fear you might not really know what you fear the most, so that might be a very good answer. I think you have had family troubles, maybe an abusive father but you just do not realize it. Oh look the rain as stopped" he looked out and up into the dark sky. The windscreen wipers were turned off and she pulled out onto another road, several cars had passed and she had thought of stopping and trying to dash from the car but knew she would never make it in time. Coming to terms as much as she could, with her situation she tried to keep it together and just wait for her chance, and just hope one came.

Finding it to difficult to drive and getting more and more anxious she tried to ask him to move his hand again.

"I find it hard to drive safely with your hand there, could you please move it, even just a little, please?"

"Does it bother you a stranger has his hand on your pussy then" he started to move his hand round and touch her with his fist as he held his grip fast round the grenade a slight malevolent smile came across his face.

Trying not to show her discomfort she edged as far as she could back into her seat.

"It is just difficult to drive, that's all"

"That's all, are you sure that's all, you might be getting turned on, lots of women fantasize about being raped by a stranger did you know that?"

"I don't know about that but I find it very difficult to concentrate and drive safely"

"Do you now, when I was a child I used to have two rabbits, I kept them in a hutch at the bottom of the garden, one day my dad, who was an alcoholic, decided we would have rabbit for tea, he made me kill them, skin them and gut them, he showed me how as I did it, my mother was forced to cook them and then we ate them for tea, my two rabbits, which I loved and looked after from little bunnies."

"How old were you?"

"Nine, nine years old, I was always witnessing my father beating, raping, and brutalizing my mother, but that was the norm after a while, but the rabbits, well that was just not right I thought. So I never forgave him for that"

There was silence for some time and she drove faster, she didn't know why but she started to drive faster, the rain had stopped and there were more lights along the road, she knew they were coming into more populated areas. Not really knowing what she could do but it caused a slight lift in her attitude and gave her a little hope to cling on to and keep in control. She glanced across and saw the vacant look on his face, he was remembering something and was lost in his thoughts, she felt his hand twitch and feared he would just let go of the grenade as he drifted away with his thoughts.

"So what is your name?" she said in a slightly louder than normal voice to get him back and in control of the grip in his right hand.

"Simon, Simon Pearson that is my name, with letters after it"

"What do you mean?" she asked curiously.

"Never fucking mind, where the fuck are we?" he looked out of the window and noticed houses along the distance and along the way they were heading. His right hand shifted as he swung round in his seat, it was not panic, it was not surprise, she could not put her finger on what it was but he was definitely agitated.

She drove towards the lights, trying her luck she swallowed and bit her teeth together, a glimmer of hope raced through her body and mind.

His hand moved away from her and she let out a little sigh of relief as he was no longer touching her. He peered out of the window and seemed to be looking for something, he shifted in his seat and his right hand moved completely away from her but still had hold of the grenade in it, she looked at him and saw he was facing away from her looking out of the side window. His right hand down by his right knee now away from her, and no longer between her legs. His head up against the window his attention concentrating on something outside, his gaze away off in the distance.

She slowly moved her hand down and as quietly as she could unfasten her seat belt. It clicked silently as she slowly undid it from its fastening.

She felt her heart beat faster and her breathing getting heavy, he was facing away from her, his hand was gone from her crotch and she was unbuckled from her seat. She looked ahead and saw a row of houses in front of her. She put her foot down and the car sped up, he slowly turned his head and smiled at her. It sent a shiver down her spine but she kept going. Somehow theses houses were her salvation, her escape and she was heading for them. He lifted the grenade up in front of his face and kissed it, then looked back across at her, before he said calmly.

"Harriet, or whatever your fucking name is, I will always be with you, I will always be in your memory. No one or nothing can ever erase that, so in a way I am immortal."

She opened her door and in a panic and desperate survival drawn action threw herself out and landed on the road, the car veered off and out of control across the road, wasting no more time she got to her feet and ran as fast as she could not looking back.

The houses in front of her were getting larger and larger; she laughed a nervous and broken laugh as she ran faster.

She never even looked back when the explosion erupted inside the car, which had ditched in the side of the road.

The grenade obliterated the vehicle and all that was inside of it, she pounded on the first door she came to and cried and shouted in sheer panic until it was opened, lights were coming on in the other houses as the blast got the attention of the owners, the car was in flames and the street was alive with activity.

It was some days later when she was in the room with a female police officer and inspector that she was told who the man she had given a lift to was.

"He was a well respected psychotherapist for some years, until his wife was found half mutilated and decomposing in his house, he disappeared and must have been on the run for several days" The inspector was telling her, but she didn't listen, she was not even in

114

the room, her thoughts were elsewhere and the memory of the man she had picked up in the rain that night, the nice looking man with a friendly smile and blue eyes, the man who would never leave her memory.

She felt the hand on her arm and looked around. It was the police woman who smiled at her saying in a friendly voice.

"We have a councilor, who will help you if you want someone to talk to?"

"No, I don't want to talk to them; I never want to talk to them." she shook her head and pulled her hand away. She would always have this maniac with her in her head and memory. He was right in a way he was no immortal.

The End

# I WILL NEVER LEAVE YOU

It had not been right for some time and she knew it, the relationship had been going downhill since his mother died over eighteen months ago. She did love him once but now it was more pity, well that was what her best friend kept telling her. He just was not the same man she knew all those years ago. He had no happiness, no get up and drive, all he did was sloth about and had no interest in anything anymore.

She put her coat on and was due to meet her friend for a coffee. It was a great chance to get out of the house for a while. She walked into the living room where he was sat, just looking out of the window and seemed to be miles away with his thoughts.

"Ok Paul I am off, I won't be long" she said coming up to him and kissing his cheek, he turned, weakly smiled at her and kissed her back. She smiled back at him and headed out of the door.

"I will never leave you" he said to her as she left.

Driving down the road she was looking forward to meeting her old school friend, they had been inseparable at school and luckily stayed in touch all their adult life. She was like a sister she never had and they enjoyed each other's company immensely. She was someone she could tell anything to and would always be there for her, it worked both ways.

It was always the same cafe they met and they always ordered the same thing, whoever got there first ordered for the other one. It was her turn today and she sat and ordered their drinks and treats, which was a Belgium Bun. She didn't have to wait long until she saw her little friend come in, smiling and looking at her through extra wide rimmed glasses. She walked up and they hugged and sat facing each other.

"How are you my dear" her friend said smiling big like she always did.

"I am fine and how are you my good friend?"

"Oh you know, in need of a cup of ambition and a dose of happiness" she smiled and took a sip of her coffee.

"You are always bloody happy, you smile every minute of every day"

"That just puts people into a false sense of security, no one really knows what I am thinking" she winked her eye and took a bite of her Belgium Bun.

"I know what you are thinking, you are thinking about that new man who has moved into your apartment complex, you never shut up about him last time we spoke. So tell me have you been there yet?"

"Been there, what do you mean my girl, just because he has an ass so tight it would bounce off the bloody wall" she said with a mischievous grin.

"You bloody have, you are such a tart do you know that?" they both laughed and so their conversation started and they would have a few more coffees before they were done and had a good catch up. The conversation turned to her husband eventually as it always did.

"I don't know he has just changed so much since his mum died, he just cannot get over it, all the life has drained out of him,

118

no spark anymore" she said with sadness in her eyes staring at her half empty coffee cup.

"I am sorry but you need to get it sorted out, he cannot wallow in self pity forever, you have a life too. It is selfish of him to drag you down like that this is not what you signed up for"

"I know, but I feel sorry for him, he was very close to his mum and when she died he blamed himself somewhat, we just didn't have the room to take her in and she needed full time care" she sighed and took a drink of her coffee.

"Wow girl this is not you, do not start blaming yourself, he needs to bloody man up and get over it, we all lose someone, it is life. No one lives forever."

"Yes I know, but he is acting strange lately, keeps saying "he will never leave me" I don't really understand what he means. He doesn't do anything anymore, he spends a lot of the time in his garden shed, and when he comes into the house he just sits there, looking blankly out of the window."

"It is not healthy or normal, he needs help obviously, he is depressed and depression is a very dangerous thing, he will bring you down with him."

"I have talked to him about it, he just says he is not depressed and refuses to see anyone"

"Bloody hell, it would drive me mad, how long has it been now, two years"

"Eighteen months, he blames himself and finds it very hard to come to terms how she died in that home it use to rip him open sometimes when he thought about it. Then he just went quiet and then this all started, not talking, spending all his time in the shed, staring out of the window and lately he keeps saying that he will never leave me saying?"

"Well you are my best friend and I need to tell you, get him help or leave him, because one way or another he will pull you down and you will end up just like him. Depressed people are like social vampires they drain you of your energy. No matter what you do it will not help them, he needs professional help and probably some sort of medication."

"I still love him and just want him back as he was" she said worried.

"Well please think about it, you go see someone and see if you can have him sectioned or something, somewhere they can help him. I think he has to be a danger to himself or others to get that done but you could say he is causing you depression too. You have to look after yourself and not live the only life you have for someone else who let's face it, looks like shit lately, he is not looking after himself and it is just not fair on you." Her friend was genuinely concerned. They left the cafe a short time later and hugged each other. They always kept in touch by phone and would talk every day. They made plans for their next meet the week after and parted. She drove home and thought a lot about what her friend had told her. She knew deep down she was right and something had to be done. They could not go on like this and she had to tell him. Pulling onto the small driveway she saw him walking from the back garden shed. She parked up and walked in. He was now sat in the chair again and looking back out of the window.

"Paul we need to talk, this cannot go on, you need help and you are just falling more and more into depression" she said to him while standing over him looking down, her hands on her hips. She didn't get any response for a short while then he looked up at her his eyes looking tired and his face expressionless.

"I will never leave you" is all he said then looked back out of the window.

"You cannot go on like this, I cannot go on like this, it is pulling me down and not doing any of us any good" she raised her voice and became more demanding.

"I am not depressed, I am not anything, I will never leave you" he said again in the same monosyllabic way. She could feel herself boiling with anger and frustration as she looked down at the pathetic figure in front of her.

"Yes you are depressed and it is making me the same way, you might not be leaving me but I might be you if you carry on, just go

122

talk to someone" she became agitated and could see he was not listening, she knew it was no use and stormed out of the room.

Nothing more was said that day, something she had become use to, she waited for him to go out to the large garden shed later that night and then she rang her friend. They had a long talk and she needed the welcoming voice to not only talk to her but also someone to listen. She was coming to the end of her patience.

She went to bed early to end this day. Before she got into bed she looked out the bedroom window into the back garden, she saw the light from the shed still on and knew he was still in there. She shook her head and sighed out, she was past caring anymore.

She woke alone the next morning and could see the bed on his side had not been slept in. She got out of bed and went to the window, the shed was still open. She got dressed and went downstairs. He was in the kitchen with a cup of tea, sitting quietly at the table.

"Good Morning" he said turning to look at her.

"Morning, where did you sleep last night, do not fucking tell me you slept in the shed?" she said annoyed and frustrated.

"No, why would I sleep in the shed" he said to her, she sensed he was different but could not pinpoint why? He seemed to be talking more for one thing so maybe it was not such a bad start. She calmed herself and spoke normal to him again with no resentment in her voice.

"So where did you sleep, how are you feeling. Have you thought about what I said yesterday, were you even listening to me?" she came and sat across from him.

"You have nothing to worry about, I am never going to leave you" he said then stood up and left the room, but as he walked past her she could smell an odor she had not smelt before. It was not nice and she pulled a face at it.

From that moment on she knew something was very wrong, he was not the same and as the days went by he began to have this odor and it was getting stronger and stronger. She told him to get a shower and told him they needed to get things sorted out. He

124

stopped eating; he stopped showering and kept repeating he would never leave her.

She rang her friend and they arranged to meet same place as before. She drove there and was worried. It showed and her friend saw it straight away. They sat down with their drinks and no sooner had they done so she just had to spill it all out what she had been holding inside.

"I am sorry it is such short notice but I am really worried" she started to say.

"Listen no matter what it is, we can work it out and sort it out, you can come live with me I have told you that if need be, you have nothing to worry about"

"Thank you so much, I am beginning to get very worried, I do not know what to do anymore" she took a drink of her coffee and took a deep breath. Her friend could see something was very wrong and wanted to help in any way she could.

"Tell me, you can tell me anything what has he done, has he hurt you?"

"NO, no nothing like that, he just doesn't eat anymore, he smells horrid, won't shower, there is horrid smell like cat piss in the house I do not know what it is. And all he says to me is He won't ever leave me" she was shaking as she put the coffee mug down on the table.

"Listen to me, you are coming to live with me, this is bad, very bad obviously he is losing his mind and probably gone clinically insane by now"

"No, no it's nothing like that" she protested.

"Yes it is, just that. This is not normal behaviour, it is dangerous behaviour. You have to get out of that place, firstly for your own safety and secondly to save your own sanity.

"Yes" was all she said and she started to cry and sob. Her friend came round and put her arm around her and comforted her. She held her and calmed her down ignoring the looks they got from a few other customers. When she had regained her composure she sat back down and held her hand across the table.

"Look obviously it has gone beyond repair, he is losing his mind and needs help, you have tried and no one can say you have not, but you must think of yourself now"

"You are right, I am scared to even be in the same house, the smell is overwhelming and he is looking worse each day, I just cannot take it anymore."

"Right no time like the present, we are going back and you are packing your things to come live with me for a while until we sort out what to do. If he is not going to get help you get what is yours and start again, you only have one life, so live it. You cannot waste it on the dead because that is what he is" she felt for her friend but both of them knew she was right.

They drove back in separate cars and parked up, they both got out and together holding hands they went into the house. The smell hit them right away, it was a pungent strong smell and it burned the nostrils, never had they ever smelt anything like it before. Going straight up stairs they began to pack. They didn't know where he was and they didn't really care at this stage. Coming down the stairs she grabbed a few more things from some drawers.

"Just get the essentials we can come get your other stuff later, you need to get what you immediately need then we are gone, fuck it stinks in here how did you put up with this" she said holding her nose. They could not see where he was but the shed door was open and there was no other place he could be. She gathered all her things and they put them into the two cars. They were ready to go when she saw him come from the shed and walk towards the house. Her friend pulled at her to leave but she resisted.

"I am just going to tell him what I am doing, it is only right he knows"

"NO, just let's go you can ring him, he is dangerous and why the fuck is he in that shed all the time anyway?" she looked over and saw the door was left open.

"I won't be long, I promise" she walked back into the house. Her friend sighed and cursed under her breath, she knew it was a stupid idea. Curiosity got the best of her and she decided to take a look in the shed while she had a few moments as her friend was telling him she was leaving. She opened the back gate and hurried across the garden towards the shed.

He was looking at her across the kitchen when she came in, she looked him in the eye and brought all the strength she had to the front and said to him firmly.

"You have not tried and not listened so I am leaving and will get the rest of my things later. I want to say I am very sorry what happened but you must move on with your life you cannot live in the past and in grief all the time. You obviously need help, you must get it or you will destroy yourself" she could see he was looking at her blankly and she knew what he was going to say before he said it.

"I will never leave you" his words were overpowered by the screams coming from the garden shed. Looking out of the window she saw he friend staggering out holding her hand to her mouth she was being sick and shaking with fright. Running from the kitchen she dashed across the small lawn to her friend who was shaking and pulling her away desperately with fear and terror in her voice.

"Go, we have to go, let's move now" she was hysterical.

Looking into the shed to see what had spooked her friend so much made her heart miss a beat and her blood run cold. Hanging there from the roof was Paul, hung by a rope and his neck broke, foam over his mouth his eyes bulged. He had hung himself and by the look of things, it had been at least a week ago. The mess on the floor was gross and the smell dreadful. Pulling back she held her hand over her mouth and she was sick over the lawn. The hammer was fast. He struck both women hard over their heads smashing the skulls. He pulled them both into the shed and hit them both again with the heavy hammer as they lay unconscious. The final blows killed them where they lay. He put the hammer back on the rack and looked at his own corpse hanging there, then looked down and said.

"My mum left me and it hurt so much, but don't worry I will never leave you."

130

The end

# WITCH HUNTER

He didn't know the area too well, but he could feel the evil in his bones. He always knew when he was getting near; the hair stood up on the back of his neck and the pit of his stomach became hollow. Whether this was a gift or a curse he was not sure, but he knew he had it, whatever it was. He had fine tuned the talent over the past few years; knowing the mistakes he had made and, more importantly, learning from them.

He was always searching for the creatures he had come to despise. He has never let them get away and he would never stop until he knew they were gone. Not knowing how many there were, he had no idea when he would be finished, but he was focused and ready to take on the evil and malevolence of these creatures until he could do so no more. He drove for several miles and then stopped, looking out over the large field. That was it, he thought, the manor house. He just knew it.

It was a magnificent building and well kept, the people there obviously had money but he was not concerned with that right now. He looked around at the barren countryside. It seemed dead. It was quiet, too quiet. No birds, no movement, no life. Yes this was it.

"Here we go again, mate," he said to Bodie, his large dog sat in the back seat, as he pulled the car off and up towards the house.

This was always the hard part, tracking the thing down to its lair. That and making people believe him, not that he blamed them if they didn't. If someone had come to him a few years ago and told him the same things that he now tells people, he would have told them to go away and multiply, just the way others tell him now, although not in such a nice way.

He drove slowly up to the large wooden doors of the house, which looked deserted and cold. He looked around carefully before he got out of his car. Stillness and silence, a classic sign, he thought. He knew it would be near, but it was not in the house, he could sense that much. He got out of the car and let Bodie out of the back. The dog looked just as intense as Ray did as he came and stood by his master's side. Ray walked up to the house, climbed two small steps and stood at the front door. He knocked loudly and waited. There was no answer. Looking around, he knocked again.

After waiting for a few minutes he tried the handle of the door, surprised to find it open. He slowly walked in and the coldness of the place cut into his very bones. Bodie stayed by his side at all times.

Ray walked to where he could hear voices, a woman in distress, and a man trying to sound confident but failing miserably. Ray crossed the open hall then stood in the doorway of the main room. He noticed a frail looking woman crying as she sat in a chair shaking and obviously at her nerves end. The man, older looking and more dominate featured, was talking down to her, making her more distraught then she already was.

"Excuse me," Ray said in a powerful and confident voice.

Turning, the man jumped back, the woman looked like she would have a heart attack there and then as she fixed her gaze on Bodie and shook with fear.

"What the bloody hell?" the man said.

"I mean you no harm. I am here to help you. I know there is one here somewhere, just show me where it is and I will get rid of it for you." he smiled and put up his hand in a friendly gesture.

"Get out, Get out!" the man shouted threateningly but unconvincingly. He was walking towards Ray but stopped at the sight of Bodie looking at him.

"Listen, I don't mean to barge in, but it is obvious it is around. Just tell me where and I will take care of it"

"Who the hell are you? Leave this house or I will call the police," the man said, moving to the phone on a table in the corner. Ray looked at the woman, who was fixated on Bodie, then motioned to his dog to sit, which he did without question. Ray thought he looked less threatening sitting. Turning his attention back to the woman, Ray tried another approach, hoping he would get through to her.

"You know, don't you? Is it nearby?" he looked at her, waiting for an answer.

"Listen, I will not tell you again." the man had become braver now as he had more distance between him and Ray.

"Okay, I will leave, but before I do, just listen. It might sound ridiculous to you, but I know what it is, or if you like, what *she* is." This got a reaction from the woman. She stared at Ray with hurt and fear in her eyes. The man came and stood next to her, looking from Bodie to Ray.

"Who are you? What do you want?"

"That's not important right now. Just listen to me for a moment, please. I know she is around here and I know she is about to explode. She is nasty; she will destroy everything within her reach and take everyone with her. You must, at all costs, keep away from her. Do not make any contact with her. I can sense her, feel the evil. She must be gotten rid of."

136

"I do not know what you are talking about. Now please leave."

Ray ignored the man and looked at the desperate-looking woman. This is where he was going to get the information he wanted and he knew it.

"My son," is all she said before dropping her head in shame.

"Victoria that is enough, now you get out" he said pointing to Ray, who took no notice.

"Your son is involved with her?" He looked at the women and never let his gaze leave her, forcing her to meet his eyes.

"Yes," she nodded her head and started to cry. "Yes, yes."

"He is in grave danger and he must get away from her; she will destroy him and all around him. I can see she has already started here. Let me help you, before she rips his insides out, leaving him an empty shell. She will take his life force that is what she does."

Looking up at Ray with doubt in her eyes, the woman slowly found strength. She stood and looked defiant, with a new-found courage, and her doubt was overshadowed by her love of her son.

She was desperate and needed something to grab onto, some hope of getting him back.

"What will you do?" she said quietly.

"Give you your son back, your life back and rid this place of the evil that has settled here. You know she is evil, don't you? You know she must be gotten rid of."

"Just a minute I am not having you coming into my house upsetting my wife with this absolute…"

"Shut up, you have said too much already," Victoria said to him without looking at him.

"Tell me where she is and I will rid you of the bitch," Ray told her.

She looked at him for a long moment. She seemed to be looking for something in his eyes, and she finally spoke.

"You are a burnt-out man, a tough and strong man. Why are you doing this and who are you, where do you come from?"

"It's my vocation shall we say and yes I am burnt out love, have been for a long time. Now please, just show me where the bitch is and I will do the rest and you can have your son back."

"Victoria, we don't know who this man is. He just walks in here and says these things, how do you know you can trust such a man?" His voice was quieter and weaker, the power seemed to have shifted from him to her and Ray preferred it that way. She was going to give him what he wanted, he knew it.

"I trust him and if it gets us our son back, then you should trust him also." She never took her gaze from Ray as she was talking.

He looked back at her and saw the hurt and fear of loss in her eyes; she had suffered and was still suffering now. He was going to help that and it made him feel good.

"Just tell me where she is and I will rid you of the witch."

"What will you do? What about the consequences?" the man asked from behind his wife.

"There will be no consequences and you will never see or hear of her again, or me for that matter" Ray told them.

"What do you want? How did you know?"

"I just know, I just feel it and I just know. Look I do not expect you to believe or understand, but please try to comprehend the seriousness of this situation. Your son will die, be ripped apart from the inside out if she is not stopped. I can stop her, you will be free and have your son back, that is what you want?"

"Of course, of course it is," Victoria said to him with heartfelt meaning.

"Good. Is your son with the witch now?"

"He is never away from her; he is like under a spell."

"You don't know how right you are. Did she seem nice to begin with, pleasing and helpful? Once she trapped your son, she then changed and became a bitch from hell?"

They both looked at each other. They didn't have to say a word and Ray knew he was right. He looked around the cold, lifeless room.

"What can we do, please tell us?" Victoria had made her mind up to trust this man and his powerful dog. She was pinning all her hopes on him already.

"I need to know where she is, the layout of the building and surroundings if possible. I also need to know what your son looks like. Lastly, I need for you to keep quiet about all this and mention me to no one."

"Yes, of course." Victoria seemed to have a glimmer of hope in her eye. She turned to her husband, who was shaking his head, then and took his hands in hers looking him straight in the face.

"Victoria, you cannot be serious." he said.

"Give the man anything he wants, I want my son back, my life back and rid of the evil bitch that has caused us so much upset and pain. She is killing this family, killing my son, our son!" she shouted at him and he gulped with apprehension. He could see he had them, could see the desperation of these people and it was to his advantage. They had been through too much and wanted rid of the witch in any way possible.

Victoria turned back to Ray and nodded a yes. He thought he even saw a slight smile and spark of hope in her eye.

"Okay, is it alright if we clean up and wash then we can discuss what will happen?"

He and Bodie had a shower and got freshened up. It felt good to wash the days of travelling and hunting away. Ray shaved and felt better for the experience.

Their meal was made for them and it was a magnificent table for them both. Their hosts were perfect and Victoria seemed a different woman. Her husband even came around and was no longer hostile. Ray did find it a little surprising, but it was to his advantage so he didn't complain. After eating he got ready, gathered the information he needed and checked that he had the information right; the place, the surroundings, the photo of the son.

"Thank you for your hospitality. I will now rid you of this witch and be on my way. You have done the right thing, but please tell no one of what happens here."

"Thank you. I can't believe I am doing this, but I feel it is the right thing and you are the right man," Victoria said to him. She took his hand and held it in hers for a moment and he could feel the brittleness of her grip. He put his other hand on top of hers and said in a low voice to her, "I will not let you down and you will have your son back."

No more was said. He left them both standing there holding each other fearfully. A pathetic but desperate sight, he thought. Darkness was falling and twilight came creeping in. He now knew where the witch was, in a small house only half a mile away. It was on the same land, but down by the river. Victoria had given him directions and he decided to walk.

Taking his faithful crossbow from the car boot, he swung it over his arm, fixing a sheaf of four arrows to his leg by tying the two cords at the top and bottom. He walked to the river, followed by his dog. It did not take him long to spot the place. A small house, set back from the tree line. He knew it was right, he could smell the stench of the witch in his nostrils now. She was in there and she was a nasty one, he could tell.

Bodie came quietly to his master's side and stood, fixed and ready for any command given to him. He had become just as used to it and as professional as his master at all this. Looking down at him Ray said,

"Are you ready, old friend, another one to go?" He slowly moved off, back into the trees. He kept a slow but steady pace up to the house. It was unnaturally quiet; no birds, no sound, no life. Bodie moved beside him in a crouched position, ready for anything that came for him. Ray stopped and ducked behind a tree. The back door opened quickly, silently and he froze. Looking from behind his tree he saw nothing, and then the door shut again. He was not sure what it meant or who it was and he looked down at Bodie, who was just staring at the house. Ray took the bow and pulled the powerful cord back; he loaded it, put the arrow in the groove and settled it in his arm like a rifle. He was ready and wanted to get it over with. He looked around, trying to familiarise himself with the surroundings in case he had to give chase. He didn't understand why the door had opened then shut again, he was not sure what it meant. He just hoped that the parents had not weakened and told their son that he was coming. The lights in the house all went out suddenly and the darkness of the trees hid the house in their shadows.

"Fuck it," Ray said as he made his move. He rushed closer to the house, crossbow ready, and he was so close now he could see inside the small front window, but he saw nothing, no movement at all. He motioned to Bodie to go to the back which he did without question. He had done this many times before and did not need telling twice.

Ray peered in through the window, desperate to try and see something to give him a clue what to do next. He decided to get closer and moving slowly and silently he backed up against the wall next to the window. He carefully moved to the side and looked in. He could just make out a shadow moving inside, then his eyes adjusted to the darkness and he saw a young man laid out on the floor. There was a chalk mark around him with symbols written on the wooden floor. This must be the son, Ray thought. He looked drained and gaunt. Ray looked around the room. He could not see any other movement and the man on the floor looked drugged and out of it. Suddenly Ray's heart missed a beat and he jumped out of his skin. A hideous face appeared at the window from inside staring right at him and snarling and salivating. Her eyes pierced the air between them and burnt into Ray's very soul. She snarled and let out a horrible inhuman shriek. Ray took a few moments to compose himself. He then turned and pointed the cross bow at her and fired but she was too quick and ducked down out of the way. The arrow flew in and embedded itself in the wall. Wasting no time, Ray ran to the front door. He kicked at it and with the second kick, it gave. He rushed in and looked left to where the witch had been. She was gone. He stood motionless, simply looking around. The man on the floor was moving slightly and moaning, though Ray dismissed him. He was alive and safe, for now. Ray's main concern was the hideous thing at the window. He looked for a light switch but couldn't see one. He was breathing heavily and reloaded his bow quickly and efficiently. He raised it into position once more and started to move around the dimly lit room. The smell was burning his nostrils, it was vile and making him heave, the room seemed to be empty of the witch. He once again looked down at the man on the floor, still moving then suddenly stopped. He knew his mistake as soon as he had made it and it was too late now. He had not looked up. The most important lesson he'd learned from making the mistake before was to look up. He ducked and crouched, looking up to the ceiling. Sure enough, staring down at him maliciously was the hideous creature from the window. She seemed stuck to the ceiling, though how she was doing it was the least of Ray's worries. He lifted his bow and squeezed the trigger. The arrow flew true, but she had already begun to move and it only caught her in the arm, but enough to spin her to the left and away from Ray. The scream was deafening and Ray moved fast. He kicked out at her hard, catching her in the ribs and reeling her to the side once again. She was up much more quickly than he had anticipated, pulling the arrow out of her arm. Turning this to her own use, she ran at Ray wielding it like a knife. The point just missed Ray's face by inches as he ducked away and moved back. He used the cross bow as protection and swung it in her direction. He hit her, but it did not seem to faze her in the slightest, she brushed it aside and came for him with an insane madness. Ray dropped the bow for a moment and grabbed her injured arm. He pushed it back with all his force and then pulled it towards him, trying to pull it out of the socket. He then sidestepped and swung her. Her forward momentum took her past him and again he pulled the arm back. He heard a sickening crack as the bone snapped under the pressure and she fell to the floor, reeling in pain. Ray let go of the arm and reached for his crossbow once again. He looked up as he was loading it seeing her run to the back door, he followed. She was holding her arm limply to the side; it was broken, the bone snapped and sticking out by her elbow. She looked intensely evil as she rammed the back door, going straight through it and taking it off its hinges as she did. Once outside, she

148

started to run for the trees. Her surprise was total when teeth embedded into her leg. She screamed out and looked down at what was ripping her flesh. Bodie had been waiting and now he was doing what he had always done. She kicked at him and punched him with her other arm, trying desperately to free herself.

"Bodie, leave," Ray said from the back doorway. Instantly Bodie backed away. Ray was already aiming his arrow at her and this time, he did not miss. She turned and stumbled. The arrow caught her directly in the temple, piercing her head. The force of the blow knocked her off her feet and smashed her into the fence. The arrow impaled her to the fence, her arm was broken and her leg ripped open. Stuck as she was, she still snarled, screamed and spat at him. He just took a deep breath and looked at her, seeing the pure evil in her eyes. The horror of her form and the sight of her spewing at him disgusted him.

"Bodie, quiet her," Ray said without looking as his dog came forward to the witch who spat at him and violently tried to rip her head from the arrow holding her to the wooden fence. Bodie went for her throat, ripping and tearing at it until he tore it out. The screeching had finally stopped; she had no voice box left. Her struggle still continued for a few minutes until she died, twitching and convulsing spasmodically. Ray watched her die. He waited and looked until he knew she was dead, he knew she would never hurt anybody again, but he had to make sure. He loaded his cross bow once again and took aim for her head. He fired and the arrow entered with a sickening thud. It stuck through her head and into the fence, just like the first one had. He would come back later to burn the body, but right now he returned to the house. He looked at the pathetic sight of the man on the floor, curled up in a ball and crying, weeping like a baby. He could not be older than his mid-twenties, Ray thought. He looked down at him and said,

"Come on, son. Let's get you home to your mother."

Victoria wanted to see Ray before he left. She came out of the house as he was getting in his car to leave.

"Please, wait for just a moment," she said, coming up to him with an envelope in her hands.

150

"There will be a fire in the woods tonight. Please don't worry about it, I am just burning rubbish and it will be gone by tomorrow, okay?"

"Please stay here tonight," she pleaded.

"No. I have to finish what I started. I will sleep in the house in the woods tonight; do what I have to do, then be gone by the morning"

"How do you live?" she asked with genuine concern.

"Day by day, as they say."

"I can never thank you enough. I was not sure what the hell I was doing when I agreed to let you do this, but I wanted my son back. I could feel you were a good man, deep down."

"Save it. I have done what needed to be done, love."

"Please take this as a token of my gratitude," she said, handing him the envelope. Ray looked at it, then took it and put it into his inside pocket, saying, "Now please remember, you have not seen me. You know nothing about what happened. Please tell your son to do the same."

"Yes, I will. Thank you so much for what you have done. What was she? It is so horrible to think…"

"Well don't think then, that's the best way isn't it? Just get on with your life and forget it ever happened. You will have no more trouble from that bitch."

With that, Ray left. He drove away without looking back. He returned to the house in the woods and as he told Victoria, there was a fire that night in the clearing in the woods. He had evidence to get rid of, a witch to burn. He slept well and was up early the next morning. He first scattered the ashes and what was left of the fire he had made the previous night. Then he looked up and took a deep breath of crisp morning air. He noticed a bird singing its morning chorus and knew that life was returning to the forest, to the place where it belonged. Bodie was shaking the water from his fur as he had been playing by the river. Now he rolled on his back and scratched himself as he moved about with his legs up in the air. He looked soft and gentle, his tail was wagging and he seemed to have a grin on his face. The powerful beast was playing and enjoying this time while he could. Ray went to the car. He opened the boot and took a bag out; it had a board of some kind in it. He took this to the house and put it on the floor and sat cross-legged. He opened the bag and a yellow, old-looking Ouija board which he opened and put it on the floor in front of him. Then he took the planchette from the same bag and placed it on the board. Ten minutes later he was putting it back into the boot of the car. He called Bodie over and he came running and got into the back of the car. Ray shut the door and as he was walking back to the front of the car, he reached into this pocket and noticed the envelope Victoria had given him. He ripped open the brown envelope and looked inside. It was money, twenty pound notes. He estimated about five hundred pounds. He put it back in his pocket without expression.

He looked up and saw someone walking toward him. It was Victoria, wearing a large, warm, full-length coat. She came up to him and smiled.

"You should not be out here at this time of the morning," Ray told her.

"I wanted to see you before you went." She sounded in control and much more confident then she had the day before.

"Is your son alright?"

"Yes. He is hurt and his heart and will are broken, but I will fix that for him. I am just glad to have him back."

"That's good." He nodded and gave her a quick smile. "I must be on my way. Please tell no one what happened here."

"I will tell no one, but I must know who you are and what makes you do this. Who was that woman?"

"If I told you, you would not believe me. Let's just say the world is a better place without her."

"I saw her rip my son to pieces and there was nothing I could do about it. She was an evil woman and I wanted her dead for what she had done to us. I know that is a shameful and horrid thing to say, but it is true. She was pure evil. I had never seen so much of the devil in anyone before."

154

"Yes, she was a nasty one alright."

Victoria looked at him. She was shaking her head, trying to understand what had happened. It was too much for her to take in, but she was trying.

"Who was she?" she asked once again.

"Like you said, love, she was pure evil. The worst part is that there are more out there."

"Who are you?" She looked deep into his eyes as he felt her trying to work him out; to find his reason, to find his soul.

"It's no good looking love, you won't find answers," Ray said to her, looking straight back into her own eyes.

"You are a sad man and a strong man, a warrior. I can see it but not feel it, whatever it was that burnt you out so much. Please tell me who you are. I would like to add you into my prayers for bringing my son back to me." She folded her arms and looked back at Bodie in the car. He was staring at her and she smiled at him, and then looked back at Ray with her questions in her eyes.

"The name's Ray, Yorkshire man," he looked at her and smiled. "Take care, Victoria, and thank you for the money. It will come in handy."

"It was the least I could do. Please remember that you are always welcome here, Ray. If there is anything you ever need, please do not hesitate to ask and if I can help or give it to you, I will do so gladly. You have done something for me that no other man could have done and I will always be in your debt for that." She leaned forward and kissed him gently on the cheek, lingering for a moment before returning to her standing position.

"Thank you. I might just do that sometime. Goodbye." With that, he smiled and got into his car, started the engine and pulled away without looking back.

Victoria watched him go and saw Bodie look back at her through the rear window. She stayed motionless for a few moments, watching sadly as they drove away. Then she looked back at the house and a shiver went down her spine. She did not want to enter the place ever again and she truly did not want to know what had gone on in there either. She had her son back and that was all that mattered to her. She looked back in the direction Ray had gone, took a deep breath, turned and headed back to her house.

"Nice woman, Bodie," Ray said as he sped up out of the lane and onto the road further along. He was soon heading north, the board had given him the direction and the place, and all he had to do now was hunt down the exact location.

The beginning……..

Ray is a character in a series of Books available from lulu.com or Amazon

Please visit my web site    www.fancyacoffee.wix.com/kev-carter-books

Hidden Darkness

Sisters of Darkness

Realms of Darkness

Back into Darkness

Shadows of Darkness

Dreams of Darkness

Hunters in Darkness

Out of Darkness

Darkness Within

Darkness of Ray Sibson

Darkness

Beyond the Darkness

Depth of Darknes

Kunoichi out of darkness

# EVIL

"There was a fire, but it was caught before any real damage had been done, Mr.Deighton" The estate agent told him over the phone.

"Yes, that is what I was told, so it was not an electrical fault?"

"I assure you, everything has been checked and has the necessary certification, we cannot rent a property without it now, the health and safety regulations are very strict."

"I just want to make sure, you hear these horror stories about places sometimes, I am moving in there with my daughter and want to make sure everything is right, you understand?"

"You are covered with our insurance and in the unlikely event any problems occur, we will send someone round to fix it within twenty-four hours. If it cannot be fixed in that time for any reason, it will be made good and you do not pay your rent until it is fixed. No other estate agent round here offers this Mr. Deighton, it gives you total piece of mind." His voice was assuring and professional.

Deighton thought for a moment then nodding his head, agreed with what was being said, the deal was done there and then on the phone. He had to go into the office, sign the agreement and sort out payment details then the keys would be ready for him to move in.

The day was bright and the sun shone high in the sky, he walked with a slight urgency to his daughter's school. He was picking her up to take her for her favorite meal, Fish and Chips, she loved to sit in and have a traditional meal with her dad.

They used to do it as a family until the untimely death of her mother two years before of a brain tumor, it was devastating for them both and their lives were ripped apart. They have become closer and more dependent on each other since.

He found it hard to bring his daughter up by himself sometimes, but it was a promise he made to his wife before she died. He would look after her and make sure she was safe at all times. He stopped outside the school gates and looked across the yard, the children had already started to come out, but he knew Sian would not until she could see him arrive. She always waited inside the school until she could see her dad arrive then she would come out to meet him.

Tall for her age with short blond hair, pale but healthy complexion, she strolled out with her bag round her shoulder and smiled as she came closer; he smiled back and noticed her mother in her more each day, that childlike innocence and natural beauty that was so hard to find in women these days.

"Hi angel" he said bending down to give her a kiss on the cheek, she returned the kiss and smile then gave him a hug.

"I love you daddy, more and more each day" she said holding him tight.

"Love you too princess."

"Oh, I'm an angel and a princess today" she smiled and they walked away, she proudly held his hand and felt safe and secure while doing so.

"You want the good news, or do you want the good news?" he said as they walked along.

"Erm, the good news I think, then save the good news until later"

"Ok, we have the house and we move in this weekend, you can finally have your own room and stop sharing with your cousin"

"We have our own place and don't have to live with uncle anymore?" her eyes widened with happy anticipation beaming from them.

"Yes, we pick the keys up on Friday and can start moving in this weekend. When we get back you can start to pack your stuff up into boxes and get ready for the move"

"Fantastic, oh that is brilliant news" she held his hand tight and smiled up at him as they walked along the pavement.

"Thought you would be happy"

"My cousin snores really badly daddy, and I struggle to get to sleep sometimes"

"Well from now on you will have your own room and your own space, I want it kept tidy mind and there will be a lot to do when we move in, a lot to sort out"

"Oh yes I know, and I will love helping you with it, I will keep my room tidy, I do not do mess you know that, so what is the other good news?"

"I bloody love you so much," he said looking down at her as they strolled along.

She smiled up at him and it tugged at his heart strings to see that angelic smile she had inherited from her mother.

"I love you too daddy and stop bloody swearing" she laughed and squeezed his hand.

"Well the other good news is that it is furnished so we can just move straight in."

"Oh cool, you are the best" she laughed out with excitement and joy.

They went into the Fish and Chip shop and sat at their normal seat by the window. They liked to people watch and take the mickey sometimes. It was in fun as they had always done it and knew they would never change.

That night Sian carefully started to pack her things, her cousin was a selfish girl and never offered to help at all, both girls were glad she was moving out at last, it had been a strain staying there, the last few months had been very hard for them all.

Saturday morning could not come soon enough, Sian was very excited and could not sleep, which was not a good thing because her cousin snored and kept her awake. She always tried to fall asleep before her but it was not easy. Somehow it didn't matter now she was too excited to sleep anyway. She had thoughts how she wanted her room to look and what she wanted in it, this took her mind off the snorting noise coming from her cousin laid in the next bed to her. In a few hours it would be Saturday and they were moving to their new house, alone and with no snoring or cramped living conditions. She was thankful for her Uncle and his wife helping them out like that had, but it was all getting a bit strained now and they had begun to get on each other's nerves.

Saturday morning came and it was time for them to go, her cousin never even said goodbye, their few possessions were put in the back of the car, they had put the rear seats down and just managed to cram it all in, so one journey would do it.

They said their goodbyes and left. Driving away, they both looked at each other and sighed out at the same time, then laughed out loud.

"Right, let's go get unpacked and moved in" he said changing gear and heading off up the road.

"You are brilliant daddy, and I know we are going to be very happy here in our new home, with no snoring" she said laughing.

"And decent cooking"

"Oh yes, auntie's culinary skills did leave a lot to be desired I must say"

"Well it was nice for them to put us up, so I suppose we shouldn't complain," he paused and thought for a moment, "but her cooking was bloody bad."

They both burst out laughing and could not help themselves.

"Sometimes I dare not ask what the hell it was" Sian said as she laughed uncontrollably.

"Better we didn't know I think, that woman burnt everything, so it all just looked the same and tasted of a charred sacrifice …..well actually I don't know what it tasted like?"

"Undomesticated I think the word is, I wonder why your brother married her for sometimes, don't you?"

"Well it wasn't for her cooking, that is for sure"

They both grinned and felt good, it was going to be a fresh start and something they both needed as it had not been an easy time after the death of his wife. They needed this house as a building block and new way of life.

He pulled up outside the modest two bedroom detached house and stopped. He looked up at the stone-cladding which ran across the building and waited for the reaction of Sian. She looked at the house, then up and down the road, she turned and smiled at him saying,

"I love it, it looks really nice dad." She got out of the car and stood staring up at the house that was to be her home from now on.

He got out and locked his car; he walked on and up to the house, followed by his eager daughter, excitement in her eyes and a bounce in her step.

Turning he looked down at her, as he put the key into the lock.

"Are you ready?" he asked.

She nodded and was eager to explore the inside. He opened the door and they both walked in. It was a welcoming house, clean and tidy; the place was modestly furnished and looked homely. They both stood looking round the room, the wooden banister that led to the upstairs, the door to the right which was the kitchen, the marble effect fireplace to the left, windows looking out to a small garden on the back wall.

Sian looked round and got a feel for the place, she closed her eyes and just stood there for a moment, listening and feeling the atmosphere. Deighton walked past her and into the kitchen, he had been earlier and got some essentials like milk and tea bags, at least they could have a cuppa now they were here.

"Going upstairs daddy" he heard his daughter shout, then the sound of feet running up the wooden stair case. He left her to find her way and explore the house for herself; he made some tea and looked out of the back window into the small garden. His thoughts drifted to his late wife. The way she used to tend to their garden, the way she used to love planting things and nurture them to grow.

After looking at the toilet, and main bedroom at the front of the house, Sian looked into the airing cupboard and across the small landing, her excitement showed on her face; she liked this house and the freedom it would give her away from her cousin and uncle. She finally ended up in the back bedroom; this was going to be her room. She imagined, with it being the smallest. A single bed and small set of drawers beside it, a wardrobe stood unobtrusively in the corner, some shelving and a small radiator on the far wall. The curtains were open so she walked to the window. Looking out across the garden to the house across the way, she scanned the area and smiled to herself. Turning she looked round the room, it was her space, her room, the far wall was bare, it looked empty and cold, but she would soon change that. She already had ideas to where she was going to put things and the layout she was going to have, the posters she wanted up on the walls and the small lamp she wanted by her bedside.

"Sian, teas up" she heard her dad shout from downstairs a few minutes later, she skipped out of her new room and down the stairs. The room was empty, silent, the door was ajar, but slowly it began to open steadily and rocked open wide, before stopping abruptly.

After they had had their tea, they began to unpack the car, moving all their things in and putting things away, they both knew what they had to do and just got on with it. Clean bedding was put on the beds, things stacked away in the kitchen, clothes put in wardrobes, and personal belongings found new places to sit.

It was busy but they both enjoyed it. As Deighton was putting some clothes away he looked out of the bedroom window and saw a small elderly woman. Stood on the other side of the road looking up to the house, she noticed Deighton and just stared at him blankly. She had sadness in her eyes and a lived in face, emotionless, she stared for a few moments then took her gaze away as she moved on up the road not looking back. Deighton watched her go; he thought she must be in her seventies, then paid her no more attention and carried on with what he was doing.

The day went quickly and they got a lot done, both were tired but had enjoyed their tasks and it was all the more fulfilling doing it together.

Before they knew it, the darkness had fallen and it was mid evening. They had been working all day and eaten in between. Deciding to go to bed they turned out all the lights, locked the door and headed off up the stairs. Sian brushed her teeth and went into her room, closing the door behind her shouting a good night as she did.

Deighton washed his hands, face and brushed his teeth. He looked at himself in the mirror, deep into his own eyes, he missed his wife and the companionship he had with her. The special bond you have when you find your soul mate, that time you find your perfect partner. The most important thing in his life now was his daughter. He wanted to give her the best he could and would make sure nothing or no one stood in his way, or her happiness.

Their first night was uneventful, they were both more tired than they realized and fell to sleep almost instantly.

Sian woke the next morning and opened her eyes, she rubbed them and waited for that few moments for them to focus. She looked round her room and smiled, her very own space, her very own world.

She stretched out and yawned, then lifted her body to sit on the edge of the bed; she had a small tee shirt on and nothing else. She looked round the room then suddenly felt strange. She frowned and looked round to every corner, she was alone but felt as if someone was watching her, staring, she could feel their eyes looking at her. She folded her arms and hugged herself, shaking it off as she stood and got dressed.

He father was already up and cooking some bacon, she smiled and her eyes widened at the smell as she came down the stairs.

"Good morning wonderful father" she said going to the fridge to get some orange juice.

"Good morning wonderful daughter, I thought the smell of bacon would bring you down"

"Oh you know me so well" she said smiling and sitting at the table.

"Did you sleep well?" he asked as he made a bacon sandwich for her and brought it over on a small plate.

"Like a log and you?"

"Like a log" he smiled and watched her face light up as she bit into the sandwich. He knew how to make it for her just the way she liked it, plenty of bacon, some brown sauce and cut diagonally not squarely. He went to get his own and he joined her at the table. After their breakfast, Sian insisted on washing up and then she went back up to her room. On entering it she instantly smelt the cigar smoke but could see nothing. She curled her nose up in disagreement at the smell, walking to the window she opened it and thought it might be coming from outside. But the day was fresh and bright, no foul smell out there. She turned back into her room and noticed the smell was subsiding; she looked around and had no idea where it could have come from. She froze for a moment when she saw her t-shirt she had been wearing was gone, she knew she had put it on the bed; she always did for the following night. It was not where she left it, she looked under the bed and all round but could not find it. Panic began to rise and she shouted for her father.

He came running up the stairs and into the room, worried and confused at her cry.

"What is it darling, are you OK?" he said looking round the room.

"Something is wrong" she said shaking her head and wondering if she had over reacted.

"What, what has happened?" he came to her and she grabbed his arm.

"My tee shirt is missing, I put it there on the bed before I came down and now it is gone, and I smelt a strange smell when I came up to my room like a horrid cigar smell"

Deighton looked around and couldn't see or smell anything but could tell his daughter was distraught somewhat.

"It probably came from outside darling, someone walking past or something?" He knew it was not convincing but nothing else could explain it. He walked and looked over her bed and then under it, there was no sign of the tee shirt. She sighed and smiled; she had calmed and felt a little foolish. The sight of her father there with her made her feel better, safer and happier.

"It will turn up I expect, sorry dad"

"Hey you have nothing to be sorry about, it is a strange house and we have to settle in and feel comfortable here so do not worry." She hugged him for a long time and then smiled as he left to go back downstairs. She carried on with her room, opening the window to let the Sunday air in and continued to rearrange and sort her clothes out.

Deighton was stood in the front room looking out of the window a short time later, he again saw the woman he had seen the day before, and she was stood looking at the house again. He

174

moved and went to the front door, he made the excuse he was going to his car and when he reached it he made the point of looking at her and saying with a smile.

"Hello"

She looked at him, worry in her eyes, and pain on her face.

"Hello", she said slowly.

"I noticed you looking at the house yesterday, and today you are here again, is everything alright?"

"No, you should not have brought your daughter here, no child should ever live in this house again and it should be demolished"

"I beg your pardon?" Deighton said a little unprepared for her answer.

"If you love your daughter, leave this place and never bring her back to it." She looked at him with sadness in her eyes and with urgency in her voice.

"Look, I do not know who the hell you are but don't start with this kind of crap with me, you won't scare me off and you will be sorry if you try, what the hell are you saying and who the hell are you anyway?" Deighton said angrily.

"I live at the end of the next street in a bungalow, you cannot miss it, all the neighbors call me a witch and an old hag, but they have no idea, I know what went on in this house and you are going to have to get your daughter out and safe because if you don't….."

She was not allowed to finish before he forcefully butted in on her.

"Right listen to me, I do not know who you are and I do not care, I'm an easy going bloke, but don't you ever come here to my house again, don't you ever speak to my daughter, it will be a fucking sorry day for you if you try." Deighton frothed with anger and stared at this woman in front of him. She said nothing and just shook her head; she slowly turned and walked away, her head bowed and her fragile frame being carried on her not too strong or stable legs. He watched and as his anger subsided, he felt sorry and regretted swearing at her. She did not look back and he watched her turn the corner at the end of the street and was gone. He sighed and looked round the place, it was Sunday and quiet, not many people about and nothing strange, he looked up at the house and thought for a moment about what she had said. He dismissed it and went back in.

It was late, almost midnight when he heard the screams. He bolted up in his bed, startled and not sure if it was a dream. He listened while breathing heavily, his eyes widened with fear as he heard the terrified scream of a young girl and a raspy deep laugh from a man. He dashed from his room and bolted to Sian's room as he burst in and looked at his daughter. She was fast asleep and calm, the room was empty and still, the screaming had stopped as he looked around frantically.

It was still and silent. He looked at his daughter quietly sleeping in her bed, the window slightly open and the curtains gently moving in the night breeze. He sniffed and smelt the cigar. He looked round once again and saw nothing.

Walking to the window he looked out into the street, it was empty and quiet, he turned back into the room and the smell had gone.

Taking another look round he quietly left the room and went back to his bed. Putting it down to a bad dream he laid there, but was unable to get back to sleep, he listened for the rest of the night and even went to check on Sian a few more times before she got up. He said nothing to her about what had happened and she was none the wiser.

Her school day went good, her father picked her up from the gates, they drove home in a happy mood and he said nothing to her. He hid his concerns well.

They both entered the house and settled down for a much wanted cup of tea before going to get changed. Deighton listened as Sian went to her room, she was quiet in there and came back out a few minutes later changed and smiling.

He was relieved, and just went up himself for a shower. He smiled and shook his head, it must have just been a bad dream, his mind playing tricks on him as he felt a little foolish at thinking it could be anything else. He was tired from being up most of the night and enjoyed his shower, it seemed to revitalize him and make him feel much better.

Sian read a book while Deighton did a little work he had brought home, the night went quickly and they both had an early night.

Deighton lay in bed and listened. He had left his door open and could hear nothing. His daughter was safe in her room and nothing was in there, he had checked. The ranting of an old woman was not going to bother him. The smell just came from outside, it must have done. She just misplaced her tee shirt, it will turn up. A new house, strange place, his mind playing tricks on him, hearing things, smelling things, he smiled at the absurdity of it. Turning over he pulled the covers over him and closed his eyes.

The night was still and the house was quiet, both Sian and her Father were asleep. Neither of them heard the low toned laugh, the smell of the cigar. Sian was unaware of the sheets being slowly pulled from her body as she lay asleep. Her young body sprawled out and her tee shirt lifted high. The shadowy figure stood above her, the foul smell coming from his breath, the cigar gripped in his teeth, the old dirty clothes he was wearing, the lust in his eyes as he looked at her young body. He began to chew on the cigar, covetousness on his face looking at her laid there below him. An evil growl emanated from his throat. His eyes widened as he stared at her.

None of them knew how long he was stood there or where he came from, he had gone the next morning and Sian woke chilly with no covers on her; she crawled out of bed and rubbed her face, got dressed and paid nothing in her room any notice. If she had looked more closely, she would have noticed her clothes had been searched through and her drawer slightly opened where she kept her underwear.

She went to school totally unaware she had been looked at most of the night in her bed. Deighton dropped her off at school and came back home, he was taking the day off that was owed to him. He drove back and came round the corner to see the old woman once again on the pavement looking at the house.

He stopped the car and got out walking up to her, he was about to speak but she spoke first saying positively.

"He is back, the cigar chewing bastard is back, and he is after your daughter"

Deighton looked at her as she stared at him; she could see the doubt in his eyes and knew something was wrong.

"Who are you talking about?" he finally asked.

"He was a pedophile who took children to this house, raped and mutilated them, just one got away and she was able to tell her father. He came down here and killed the filthy bastard in the rage and fight that followed, but he returns and must be burnt out and destroyed, this house must be destroyed"

"I want to talk with you, will you come in" Deighton found himself asking calmly, which surprised him but he seemed to have no control over it.

"No, I do not want to go into that house again, you must leave and get your daughter to leave with you" she was very insistent and almost pleaded with him.

"Where can I find out about the history of this house, about who lived here?"

"I have told you, he was an evil man, a murderer and child killer. Has something happened, what has happened?" She pulled his arm and looked deep into his eyes.

"Nothing, nothing has happened" Deighton told her pulling away from her grip.

"You are lying, he is back and he will take your girl, get her out of here. Are you stupid, are you that stupid, you cannot see what he will do."

"Who, what will who do? No one is living here except me and my daughter"

"He has always lived here; he was born here, abused by his father, disowned by his mother. You are not alone in that house, he needs to be burnt out and the house needs to be destroyed" she raised her voice and he heard the desperate fear in it.

Deighton did not know what to say or do; he didn't want to believe this woman but could not help being pulled in by what she was saying.

They spoke for another twenty minutes, she just kept repeating herself and eventually they parted, none moving ground or getting any further. He searched the house from top to bottom, searched Sian's room three times and found nothing. No one was in that house except him and the doors were locked and bolted from the inside, even if they had a key they could not get in. The words from the old woman rang in his ears, he looked on the internet and tried to find some information on the house but found nothing. There was not a library close by so he could not check there; the estate agents were no help either. All he had was the ranting of an old lady. He tried to dismiss it but could not. Again he went up to Sian's room and sat on her bed, the room was tidy and clean, nothing strange about it at all.

He sighed and went back downstairs; later he went and got his daughter from school and took her out for dinner. It was a nice treat for her and they had a good time together. It was half past nine when she went to bed, he watched her go up and listened while she brushed her teeth, then go into her room. All was silent as he locked up the house. The doors were locked and bolted from the inside and all the windows were secure; no one was getting into this house without him knowing about it.

He fell into a restless sleep that night but it didn't last long, the scream of his daughter and the evil growl that turned into a laugh woke him like a bolt of electricity through his body. He dashed into Sian's room. It was empty, the window firmly shut, the house was secure.

"Sian, Sian", he shouted and frantically searched the room and house, running round distraught and fear ridden he could not find his daughter but he could hear the deep laugh, where it was coming from he had no idea.

In an anxious bid he ran from the house and down the street, not knowing what was driving him to do it, but he turned into the next street and looked for the bungalow, he saw it and ran towards it, just hoping it was the right one.

Banging on the door he screamed out for them to open, a light came on and the window opened and a voice from behind the curtain spoke.

"Go away leave me alone" The voice was weary and full of pain.

"He has Sian, he has my daughter" Deighton screamed.

Moments later the old lady opened the door and came out, she was in a dressing gown and she grabbed him by the arms, saying to him urgently.

"There is a door in the wall in the back bedroom, it is covered up now but it goes up into the rafters where there used to be another room. She will be there, that is where he used to hide the bodies. You must be quick, go, go and kick the wall in"

Without a moment's hesitation he ran off back to his house, the old lady went back into her bungalow, only to reappear moments later with an overcoat over her dressing gown, she hurried up the street and followed him round the corner.

Deighton was breathing heavy as he blindly ran back into his house, up the stairs and into the back bedroom, Sian's room. He looked at the wall and kicked at it but nothing seemed to give. He banged it and kicked it then he heard the hollow sound, it was a false wall. This was it, he kicked and punched the wall and it soon broke. The wooden door that had been disguised behind the ply wood that was now there. The laugh echoed in his ears, the evil annoyed shout coming from somewhere, but he didn't know where, stifled the air round him.

He ripped and kicked at the wooden wall and pulled the plywood free and off. He was faced with a door, he pulled it and hit it but it was locked. He looked round in a frantic search for something, anything to get him into that locked door. He froze when he saw the old lady stood there in the doorway, she held up her hand and he saw she had a key in it. Without saying a word, he took the key from her and was not surprised when it fit the door. He opened the door, peered in and saw his daughter looking up at him from the small compartment. How she got there he was not concerned at this time. He reached down and took her outreached arm, she had a gag round her mouth and was crying, scared and shaking but she was alright. He pulled her up and brought her to him, taking off the gag, she hugged him and cried. The cry of anger filled their ears and the room shook with the noise of this vile man who had lived here. Looking at the old lady, Deighton asked.

"How the hell did you know?"

"That is where he put me when I was only six, but I got out and locked the door, I ran and told my father, I have kept the key ever since. Take your daughter and leave this house, don't ever return here."

He read that the house had been burned to the ground some weeks later, but he never told anyone about the old lady and he never told anyone what had happened. All he knew was his daughter was safe and he would never doubt the ranting of a little old lady again.

The End

# MANS BEST FRIENDS

Sheila had one more call before she finished her shift and could go home. She didn't like being a home carer anymore. Just too much is put on them and not enough time to do it. She felt so bad sometimes leaving the old folks she had to go see, some just wanted to chat. She was the only person they saw a lot of the time. This was due to the tighter rules they had been put in place, giving them a maximum of ten minutes a visit. It just was not long enough and she hated doing it. The new company who had taken over were money orientated and didn't care about the old folks she had to go see.

She pulled up outside the little bungalow and walked to the front door, there was a safe box on the wall with a combination lock on it. This had the pass key into the house, she keyed in the number, opened it, took the key and let herself in.

"Hello Walter, it's me" she shouted as she went in. She could hear Walter talking to someone when she arrived but it always stopped when she entered his room. She knew there was no one there and took it for what it was. He was a lonely old man and she felt sorry for him. He had no one and was just here by himself. He talked to himself but what was the harm in that. He always had a smile on his face when she came to see him every night and put him to bed. He was a small frail looking man with just a scraping of grey hair on his head. He smiled at her but had no teeth; she always gave him a smile back. She made sure he had taken his medication then she put him to bed every night.

"How are you today my lovely?" he said to her as she was getting him ready.

"I am good Walter, how are you tonight, do you need the toilet?"

"Doing the best I can, that is all you can do, I have my lads so we are good" he looked over to one of the many photos he had scattered about of two large Alsatian dogs.

"You loved those dogs didn't you, do you need the toilet?" she said undressing him.

190

"Oh I still do, they are very loyal you know. Man's best friend, much better than humans I would say, not meaning you of course you are lovely. No I don't need to go thank you" he grinned a toothless grin at her.

She smiled back at him and lifted his small frail figure up and into bed, easing him down she made him comfortable. Then looked round and made sure everything was well. She wrote in the log book what she had done and the time. Taking his medication she went and got a glass of water then coming back over, she sat on his bed and looked at him. His little face looking back at her his eyes full of love but also full of pain because of his condition. She made sure he took his tablets and then settled him down.

"Thank you, I will remember you don't worry, I have my money and I will give it to you"

"I don't want your money Walter, have you no family?"

"No love I don't, everyone is gone, I out lived everyone, but I have my lads so I don't get too lonely with them around" he smiled at her. She had stopped asking what he meant a long time ago, she knew he talked to himself and had heard him just about every time she came.

"Well I hope you are happy Walter, you are a lovely man" she smiled at him and squeezed his little frail hand in hers.

"I have all my money hidden in a box, it is here but hidden" he said in a low voice.

"No, you should put any money you have in the bank. It will be much safer; I wouldn't tell anyone if I was you about hidden money Walter there are a lot of dishonest people about"

"Oh, don't worry my lads will take care of me" he looked over at a photo of his dogs on the wall and nodded with a smile on his face.

She felt sorry for him and knew this fantasy of his old dogs was all he had to keep him going. She stayed another ten minutes seeing it was her last call then she left. Locking the door she put the key back in the key safe and went home.

Her new boy friend was waiting for her and pounced on her as soon as she got in. She loved the attention but was just so tired she had to push him off.

"I'm sorry, I am just so knackered" she smiled and walked past him into the kitchen.

"That's fine, I just want you all the time baby" he said watching her take her shoes off.

"That's nice, why not make us a cuppa while I go get changed" she said smiling at him then headed off upstairs. She came back down a few minutes later in a dressing gown and snuggled up on the settee with her boy friend. They had only been seeing each other for a month but she welcomed the attention she got from him. Her last husband paid her none and she got tired trying to get some from him. She had been alone for some time after they divorced but this new boy friend, although much younger was nice and gave her the attention she craved.

"How was your shift?" he asked as she snuggled back into him and he put his arms round her.

"It was good, just feel sorry for them sometimes, poor old folk just left there and some have no one, it is sad, and these new bloody rules they are enforcing on us are fucking ridiculous, they give us more people to visit and less time with each one"

"It is all down to money, most things are these days, these poor buggers have nothing and no one, so they look forward to you visiting I bet"

"Yes, Walter was talking to himself again when I went there, don't know who he is chatting to but it keeps him happy so why not" she sighed.

"Like you say they have no one and nothing" he seemed genuine with his response.

"Well Walter said something funny tonight, said he is leaving me all his money, and says he has it hidden there" she shook her head and sighed out.

"What he has a stash of money there in the house?"

"No, I doubt it, but you never know with these people, I remember a few years ago one old man died and when they came

194

to empty the house he had thousands of pounds under his mattress and under the carpets, some old money that was out of date too so must have been there years. The fucking state takes all their savings and put them into care. It is wrong the whole fucking system is wrong" she became agitated and annoyed.

"Hey, calm down baby" he gave her a hug and she welcomed it.

"Anyway where is my bloody tea?" she said smiling at him.

The next day while she was taking a shower her bag was carefully searched, her note book looked at and an address and key number remembered. He put it all back carefully and she was none the wiser. He had what he wanted now, the address and the entry code for the key. He now had the potential of a lot of easy money, he was not here for the long term and knew he would be gone soon; he had grown bored of her and wanted to move on, this money he hoped was there for the taking would give him a chance to do that. He had the address and he had the times this old man was left alone, no one visited him after the morning visit until lunch time so he thought against a day light raid. The night would be better he thought that way it gave him enough time to get away and under the cover of darkness.

That night he had made some excuse to her that he could not come round as he was not feeling well, she believed him. He was actually parked not fifty feet away when she left the house and watched her leave. He gave it five minutes then headed over to the house.

He had the number for the key and he quietly let himself in. It was dark and he could hear the old man talking, he stopped for a moment and listened.

"That's it lads, you sit there, there is nothing to worry about, you are good boys you never left me, I knew you wouldn't"

He had no idea who he was talking to but he put on his ski mask then went into the bedroom and turned on the light. The old man was sat up in bed looking down to the floor when he barged in. He startled him and the look of fear on Walter's face was paramount.

"Listen you silly old fucker, give me the money and no one gets hurt, I take it and I am gone, so where is the money you have stashed" he shouted.

"What, no, I have no money son, please, just leave me alone" Walter was scared and felt helpless, scared and he began to shake.

"Where is your money" he came up to Walter and grabbed him violently by his night gown twisting his fist so it tightened round his neck. He could feel how weak and helpless this old man was and how much he was shaking with fear.

"Please, please just leave, I do not have any money" Walter spluttered out.

Throwing him back violently onto the bed, he searched under the bed then lifting the mattress almost throwing Walter onto the floor. He looked round and ransacked the place but could not find any money anywhere. He stormed back into the bedroom and saw Walter sat up looking at him with a sudden calm in his eyes.

"You better tell me where the fucking money is old man" he shouted at him in a very violent and threatening way.

"You need to leave, the lads won't like you doing this" Walter said.

"What fucking lads?" he looked around and noticed the photos of the two dogs. He went and knocked them off the wall and stamped on it smashing the glass and frame.

"You should not do this, they won't like it" Walter said in a raised voice.

Turning back he walked to the back of the room and knocked the other photos off the wall then turning he froze and just stared at the sight he saw staring at him from the door way.

Two large Alsatian dogs looking at him snarling, growling and hair up on their back, he gasped and backed up against the wall. They walked slowly towards him and kept him at bay.

"Back them off, back them off" he shouted at Walter who was sat up looking at him.

"You have upset the lads, they are not happy I told you, now they are going to walk you round the house and you are going to put everything back as it was"
198

The two dogs manoeuvred round and shadowed him and moved him about the house, they guarded him as he put everything back he had thrown about looking for the money. He was shaking and scared, the dogs were very professional. One guarded the door as the other one walked him about. He put everything back and then was edged back into the bedroom. Walter sat up in the bed and watched him tidy everything back as it was. The pictures he had smashed were just placed on the side. He stood at the bottom of the bed shaking as the two large dogs stood next to him growling low and baring their teeth.

"What, what now?" he said shaking with fear.

"Now, I should have the lads rip you to pieces, tear you limb to limb, I have seen it happen before and it is not a pretty sight. I was in the services son and I have seen a lot, I fought for this country and for wankers like you, so you can live in a free country. Why did I bother I ask myself, why are there people like you, walking around?"

"I am sorry, sorry" he said not dare looking down at the two dogs by his side.

"But you see you are not sorry, you would have had no regret at all after you left here, left me for dead it would not have bothered you. Scum is what you are; ungrateful, spoilt, selfish scum. Take your mask off" Walter said staring at him.

He did what he was told and held it in his hand like a little school boy about to be told off. He could hear the growl of the two dogs. He swallowed and could not stop the shaking taking over his body. Walter just stared at him for a moment. Then he looked down at his dogs. Each in turn his expression didn't change.

"Please, I am sorry please"

"Shut up, how did you get in here?" Walter asked.

"I took the number from my girlfriend, Sheila"

"She seems a nice woman, did she know about this?"

"No, she has no idea I am here I took the key number when she was not looking"

"You don't deserve her, and you have just destroyed her trust, you make me sick I think my lads there can have you"

"No, no please, please" he started to blubber and shake more uncontrollably.

"Youth of today make me sick. I see it on the TV all the time, pathetic. We were in the forces, we fought, we risked everything and we came home to this, to fucking wankers like you who would break in and steal an old man's money and not think twice about it"

"I am sorry, I will not do anything again, just please, I "he mumbled out incoherently then looked down at the dogs and started to cry.

"Stop saying you are sorry because you are not, you are going to leave and never return to this town, because my lads will find you if you do, and this is not an empty threat son. They will find you just like they have now, only the next time you will be ripped to bits and no one will ever recognise the remains. You leave and tell Sheila nothing you go now and never return is that clear you worthless piece of shit"

"Yes, yes I am going anyway, yes" he said crying uncontrollably.

"Isn't life strange, you came in here all hard and tough, looking to beat up and rob an old defenceless man? You leave a broken piece of crap not worth pissing on if you were on fire. Get out and lock the door, put the key back, my lads will be watching and if you ever set foot back in this town you are dog meat, literally!"

The dogs nudged him out and he went and locked the door with shaking hands, the two dogs walked him to his car and watched him go. He drove fast and didn't look back he never came back to town and never told anyone about what happened.

Walter kept talking to himself and smiled his toothless smile at Sheila who was sad and down for a bit but soon bounced back as he knew she would. She was strong, not like a lot of people these days he thought.

The End

# THE CANDLE

The candle burned steady, it flickered every now and then even though there was no draft whatsoever around it. The door was locked, the windows shut and curtains drawn as the candle lit the room very dimly. The wax had dripped down the candle on one side, where it had broken out of the small reservoir that had been made by the wick burning down.

The red wax had made a pool on the old wooden table where it was stood. Where it has been stood for some time, gently burning away and slowly killing itself as its life blood, the wax had melted and flowed away onto the table.

It was the only light emanating in the small room, the only form of illumination that was available to see what had happened. The candle had witnessed it all, the argument, the torture, the killing, but it never faltered in its duty, still it stayed lit and it just burned away there on the table.

It had all happened some hours before when it was lit then placed on the table as the man and women started to argue. She did not want to stay in the room. He was insisting she did and pulled her by the hair throwing her to the ground. She fell with a sickening thud that shocked her system.

He had then begun to shout abuse at her, threatening her and spitting down at her on the floor. She tried to stand and was violently knocked back down again. Trying to fight him she lashed out but was hit and slapped hard. She was overweight and this seemed to be what the argument was about. He was shouting abuse at her about her oversize frame and state of obesity. The argument grew loud and violent. She was crying and desperately trying to stand, she found it very hard with her size and he easily pushed her back down and kept her there. He then kicked her hard in the side. She curled up in pain rolling away from him. He followed and kicked her again calling her fat, vile and other derogatory names.

Her tears were lost on him; he just continued kicking her as she grew weaker and less able to defend herself.

He was out of breath when he was done; she was sobbing and curled up like a defenseless baby. He stood over her and shouted abuse down to her. But she was not listening, her head was thumping from inside where he had kicked it, her side screamed out every time she tried to move and the retched pain in her insides when she tried to breathe, too heavy.

He looked down at her with a disgusted look on his face; he was shaking and trying to catch his breath.

There was silence for a moment, the candle flickered doing its job and just lighting enough of the dark room to make a difference, the flame going straight up and burning the wick nicely.

The sobs of torment could be heard from the floor, the face of the man looked positively evil as he stared down at her with hate, disgust and anger in his eyes.

He looked round the room, then left by the door, locking it from outside and was gone. She still could not move as the vicious attack had done some serious damage. She could not breath without the pain tearing through her whole body, her head was like a thumping jack hammer and her breathing became desperate and irregular. The fear within her made it all worse and she began to panic, causing her breathing to become more painful and difficult. All she could do was stay perfectly still, any movement hurt and caused her sickening pain. Trying to calm herself she stayed quiet and still.

The candle had burned down at least half an inch before the door was opened again, the strong smell of beer could be smelt as the man staggered in, the draft from the doorway made the candle flicker and the flame move from side to side. The door was slammed shut and the man stood there swaying. He walked over to the woman on the floor and dropped to his knees, she shied away from him in fear as he tried to reach out to her. He became angry and pushed her away from him grunting as he did. She cried out in pained anguish, this angered the man once again and he began to shout obscenities at her saying she was fat, overweight, and had ruined his life and that she was lazy.

His final brutal assault was ferocious and nasty, he hit her, punched her and kicked her, she was quiet and still halfway through his barrage of feet and fists, but he kept going with his onslaught of violence. When he had done he dropped to the floor exhausted. He eventually staggered out of the room several minutes later. It had been still and quiet ever since. The candle still burned but was now very small and would not be lasting much longer. It flickered and faltered as it got smaller and would soon extinguish itself. The room would be in darkness then and whatever happens after, the candle would not be part of, but in its short life it had served its purpose well. It had not gone out and had burned constantly lighting the small room so the people could see what they were doing and what was happening. It had now come to the end of its life, flickering a few last times, it died and was gone. It had not been cognizant of what had happened but had been a silent witness nonetheless.

The End

Printed in Great Britain
by Amazon

26147673R00118